THE SILENC

Producer & International Distributor
eBookPro Publishing
www.ebook-pro.com

THE SILENCE AFTER THE STORM
Aliza Klebanov Florenthal
Copyright © 2023 Aliza Klebanov Florenthal

All rights reserved; No parts of this book may be reproduced or transmitted in any form or by any means, electronic or mechanical, including photocopying, recording, taping, or by any information retrieval system, without the permission, in writing, of the author.

Translation: Seree Zohar
Contact: alizaflorenthal@gmail.com

ISBN 9798865305828

THE SILENCE AFTER THE STORM

Aliza Klebanov Florenthal

*This book is dedicated to Bobbeh Frieda,
who I never had and for whom I never was.*

NEVER-ENDING

*The short distance between the sugar cubes
and crematoriums.
The distance between the house
and the barbed wire fence.
The distance between the warmth of home and
the chill of a memory, the remnants after it all,
as if it has come to an end.
Go figure, the ever-shorter distance between the
one who remembers and that which is forgotten,
between a grandfather and a granddaughter.
The distance that broadens between the
seemingly living and the dead.*

KADDISH, IN LIEU OF A PROLOGUE

Not everything has an ending. Countless things are left unresolved, much like puddles that don't evaporate in the Lithuanian summer. The images in the puddles' reflection are reversed: the homes are upside down, roofs on the bottom, gates at the top, wind vanes below, gardens above, people walking on their hats, and only the Magen David remains unchanged. But, once again, I'm making noise, cock-a-doodle-doo, gob-gob-gobble, putting the cart before the horse.

I wanted to share the pre-war times, the good times in our family, in a small house in a small town near Kovno, nothing of which remains.

They said that I ate from the table. That's true: I'm relatively tall. And when hunger gnaws, I also eat under the table. And believe me, I found good stuff. They claim that we turkeys are ugly and stupid and only one fate befits us. Me, personally, I had some good luck, though I was brought into the family for a clear purpose. I shiver when I think of it. I ran about, here, there, and into the kitchen. Frieda was standing at the counter. She gazed at me, as though eye-to-eye. A defining moment: my whole life flashed before my eyes, each situated on the side of my head. I was saved from death.

Frieda decided that, for now, I'd stay home and not be taken for slaughtering. And that's how one morning I became a member of a family that loved me like their child; well, that is, everyone other than the Rabbi. Rabbi Haim initially had his reservations but later smiled when he saw me. Thanks to Frieda, I stayed there in the family for years, long enough to get their vibe. I turned into a Lithuanian turkey. With my cumulative experience, I can say that you don't come across this kind of family every day: warm, loving, authentic, even though here and there they fibbed for the sake of domestic peace. No doubt I sound like some wise elder. But their healthy sense of humor kept me in their home. They laughed until they made me fall off the table from laughing. Frieda would laugh and cry together, wiping her tears, and then everyone would break into peals of laughter. Maybe they let me be because I was fodder for their jokes. Who knows? I don't care. I hoped to stay in that house to the very end, but I never meant that kind of end.

An end that no one could have imagined.

Cock-a-doodle-doo. Gob-gob-gobble. How grand. I'm one very lucky turkey. I've already told you that, due to my great height and Frieda's love for me, I ate right from the table - and anyone who eats with a family becomes part of it. None of my friends had the good fortune to live in homes and eat from the table. Usually we turkeys live in crowded coops, not exactly with a high quality of life, and most are brought to slaughter. Especially the sick and old ones. Very few enjoy waddling freely about the yard.

Frieda was good to me. Industrious, calm, but not very strong. Occasionally she'd sit down to mend socks or a hole in some item of clothing. She had, as they say, busy hands. Suddenly I'd see the socks dotted with diamonds. That happened only when it was just the two of us alone in the house.

The only other time there was a silence like that was on Shabbat mornings. Their sabbath, their day of rest. But on workdays, her tears blurring her vision of the eye of the needle, "Oh, oh dear, well, we can't thread the needle through tears."

I knew her so well. It saddens me to talk about her. After all, I had meant to highlight the amusing moments. But one day it was all over.

I won't put the cart before the horse. I'll let Frieda's granddaughter tell the story because, one day, Frieda became a grandmother - a Bobbeh - without even knowing it. In her rosiest dreams (and she did have many) she would never have believed that such a moment would come to pass. I mean, that someone would remember her at all, nonetheless well enough to tell her tale.

Is the tale true? Yes, for the most part. Its beginnings were sometimes comical. As for the middle part, the granddaughter, the *eynikl*, will describe that. And she, how should we put it… understands the souls of animals, like her Bobbeh. She understands me too. She paints me, and the town as well, as though she'd been there in Vandžiogala even though she's never visited. She planned to, but perhaps the eynikl is afraid of coming to a place like this which no one would want to visit. How should I know? I'm a pheasant, not a psychologist.

When the eynikl comes to Lithuania she'll be surprised. The neighborhood has changed. Instead of the butcher there's a real estate agency. Instead of the hairdresser there's a grocery store. They sell quite a bit of vodka there. Almost all the neighbors are different now too. Only one or two of the old-timers are left, and they probably can't see or hear too well. One went *meshuggeh*: stark raving mad. White-painted houses became gray; the plaster peeled. When the little houses were destroyed, new homes were built in their stead. The town conceals something horrendous. My feathers stand on edge just to think of what happened.

A little bit of the town's soul has persevered. That can't be denied. The soul can't be seen but, if one really wants to and focuses, it can be felt. And when this eynikl comes, she'll discover it; after all, she's got keen senses, just like Frieda. Truth be told, anyone who loves animals develops safety precautions, their senses sharpen. Yes, we had a special connection: Frieda admitted that she also learned a thing or two from me. She never looked down on me. One day, when she felt her eynikl writing about her, she roused suddenly. Some mighty force drew Frieda to say things she'd never have said in her short life.

I'm no turkey of good tidings. The end was dismal, that's true. The final chapters can never be denied. But, like I promised, I wanted to emphasize the beginning and the middle. The end can't be erased. It's already been recorded in the history books and preserved for posterity; yes, sure, some of which have covered up the history for, after all, how could they record the truth of what the brutal Lithuanians really did? How can one depict the true colors of those now residing in what were once Jewish homes?

I'm good with beginnings, not ends. I hid under the table when all the townsfolk quietly set out in procession, holding a child in one hand and a leather suitcase in the other. They disappeared. Into the forest. The Lithuanians knew how thick and vast the forests were. They knew that no one would hear or see what they did there. Hooligans. That's what the eynikl described. Rumor had it that the whole family was killed; and I, a member of their household, was left alone to fend for myself.

But that's not what I want to talk about. I want to accentuate the good, the tranquility; the goat wandering around the yard, a white milking goat with a smiling face, necklaced in a gold-plated copper bell; the cow pasturing in the yard; the family and, most of all, Frieda. I really have a hard time when it comes to Frieda because she was so attached to me. A wonderful woman. Not everyone saw all her positive traits. She loved reading, listening to music; she cooked well, did the laundry, sewed and did everything with dedication, morning till evening. Even when she was busy or tired or when one of the children was sick, she'd find a moment to come to me on her tiptoes, wiping her hands on her floral apron and whisper, "Oy, oy, my hyndik, I shouldn't forget you, of course I won't forget, how could I forget…"

Sometimes, when it had already become dark… after all, I slept outside, except for one night… but that's another story. It was cold, and she, dear Frieda, would bring me the leftovers of her delicious food: a scrap of meat, a chunk of potato with a bit of schmaltz and red onion, steamed vegetables, and sometimes even a herring's tail.

The Lithuanians love herring. They even eat the tail. They don't leave a single bone behind. The children play "1… 2… 3… Herring! Hide!" and the Lithuanians say, "Oh! For a chunk of bread with a piece of herring." All in small bites. The bread and the herring. And they lived happily like that, nourished by these nuggets. Of this I can assure you as I also sustained from the leftovers. They're not bad at all! And I was also privileged to enjoy some bites of carrot and ginger snaps; yes, just the once - they're hard, bitter and dry, those biscuits. Blow me down if I get why the Litvaks like them. I think they call them *teiglakh* - you place it between your teeth, then sip your tea through the air bubbles; and it makes a dreadful racket, like a storm over the ocean, but that's the only way to soften the biscuits; then they melt in your mouth. Teiglakh. They polished them off to the very last crumb. I had one once, on the family's last day at home.

Litvaks. That's what Lithuanians are called. So those Litvaks, they lived modest lives. Such a shame that they all left in convoys that summer. They all went away in one day. And I, who lived among them, understood them; in fact, over the years, I too became a Litvak. But everything's changed since then. I'm not surprised by these goyim, these non-Jewish Lithuanians.

One night… I didn't tell anyone about it but, the gate was left open by chance, "or maybe not entirely by chance," Frieda would've added, and off I flew, hovering, making a quick excursion to the center to eye the neighborhood, desolate. Nothing was there anymore, the residents, the vibrancy. Everything had gone gray, void of color, silent. I saw the sidewalks, paved with shards of gravestones. Even though I'm able to fly, I'm also close to the ground where I discovered Hebrew letters, for example P"N, initials of *Poh Nitman*, 'here lies buried.' And I found the Hebrew words *tzaddik*, a righteous man; and *eishess khayil*, a righteous woman; a *Magen David*, the Jewish star.

So, as you can imagine, I've learned a letter or two over

the years. I went all the way to the synagogue and I couldn't believe my eyes: it had been turned into a cowshed. Rumor had it that everyone had been taken, several hundred, to the heart of the forest. Lithuania's forests are vast, they're thickly wooded. From a distance, one could hear gunshots, spades, a few screams, then silence. Deathly quiet. Some Lithuanians came back to town with guns slung across their backs, chattering as though they'd just finished a day's work.

And the truth is, there really isn't any pleasure in living like this and, when my time comes, I'll accept it, bow my crest, and join my friends in the flock. They've been long since pecking at the clouds. And, like I said, the houses were all abandoned. Ours, too. It marked my end. Almost.

One day, in came Boris, thudding in his boots, husband of Maria the farmer. Oy, the way he strode in, wearing his filthy boots, throwing away the books, scriptures, the *menorah*, the candlesticks, the plates, even the special little jug for pouring water over their hands. The table and chairs and beds - those he left.

I can feel my end coming too. How do I know? Simple. I heard Boris shouting at his wife. "Look how plump this hyndik is! How long are we supposed to hang on to him? Ha? Maria. Answer me. Are you listening? Are you deaf, ha? It's costing us to keep him. What for? For his pretty little crest, Maria? What about a good roast dinner? Look at that juicy behind the hyndik's got, so plump!"

Maria gazed at me, then at him, wiped her hands on the apron and half-whispered, half hissed at him, "Plump, you potato head, oy, Boris, Boris, shut up already, you yourself are as plump as a pig." Boris didn't hear her over the crackling of the bonfire he'd made from all the books.

He stood there looking at the fire, rubbed his massive palms together, warming them. "Oy, Jesus, how good this is! There's a God, there is."

I saw the Hebrew letters blush and dissipate into the air like the finest, lightest downy feathers. There was no oxygen left in my lungs. Imagine this: it's night, at the table under which I hid Boris the Heartless sat, crude, rude and, next to him, his terrified Maria.

Well, the time has come to depart. I can feel it in my bones. I've never been as frightened as I am now. This fear paralyzes me, making it hard for me to concentrate.

I survived, and it was important for me to speak these things because truly, other than myself, not a living soul is left who can talk about the family, the neighborhood, the town. The mischievous children would ask me a thousand times: When is Purim? And I'd answer: a-dar-dar![1] Believe me, I did my best not to lose my patience.

I, who ate the crumbs under the Klebanovs' table, felt that I must say a few words, thank them for the good years I enjoyed.

But that's not what I wanted to talk about either. Rather, about the lively life that used to be, the warmth in their hearts, Frieda's two sons who left Lithuania in time. Those brothers traveled to study in France. It was their good fortune. And years later, the eldest's daughter began to tell the story. In this story, I have, at last, a place of honor. It's the only story about our town. No one else wrote about it. As for me, I was very lucky and wanted to share that wonderful period with you.

---

1. The Purim holiday is celebrated in the Hebrew month of Adar.

Even though it's possible to begin the story from the end, I promised not to twist the order around. So, towards the end of the story, I vow to make my voice heard, gob-gob-gobble, and to end with a few closing words. I won't just up and disappear, certainly not so quickly. Don't worry. It's *gurnisht*, it's nothing.

In the end, someone pulls the curtain closed.

STARTING FROM THE END

My Bobbeh, who I never had and who did not have me, was called Frieda. I'm named for her. Despite, or because, having never met, her name intertwines in mine. Now, years after her death, I understand my Bobbeh's role and recall her story. I'm building her and myself a house, thereby restoring chapters of her life that were taken from us. 'Restore' isn't really the optimal word. Nothing of it can be restored, but it's the closest I can get to the word 'revive.' Perhaps we could say 're-storied.' In the story's chapters and on the painter's canvas I can come closer to her, so to speak, though without the warmth of her embrace.

That's how I can connect.

ABBA'S MOTHER

I say 'Abba's mother' rather than 'my grandmother, my *Bobbeh*' because the deceased belonged to Abba, my father. After all, it was Abba who lost his family. I lived like one who has yet to discover something precious has been lost. The revelation occurred late in my life, years after I said, 'Abba's father' and never 'my grandfather, my *Zeideh*.' Not only have I never met him, but I hardly even heard about him. Abba, steeped in his silence, never mentioned members of his family. They seemed erased.

Once, when Abba gifted me a silver pin, he said that he'd bought it for his sister. His face showed torment; he said not a word more. Back then I'd have said "Abba bought his sister a brooch." I would never have used 'my aunt.' It was as though I'd never learned about familial relationships. As though our language, Hebrew, lacked those identifying words. Up to the age of forty I'd say, "I'm named for my father's mother." Nearing 50, I began using the Yiddish word for grandmother: *Bobbeh*; *Savta* in Hebrew. "My savta, Savta."

No one announced their arrival, no one knocked at the door,
For years, my father refused to believe
Suddenly they were all missing
I, the last remaining, write.

MISSING

Frieda is missing. For over 70 years now. There is no record of those whose lives were snuffed out. I remember my father and uncle being worried, looking, asking. The word 'missing' was felt, and unfamiliar. Years later the despair sank, like limescale in the kettle. The radio's "Relatives Search" broadcast perpetuated families' hopes, but rarely were relatives found. It brought with it more questions than answers. My father, a chemist, prepared creams for smoothing wrinkles but never made the product strong enough to remove the sediment. Now, with his family clearly exterminated, I check the elements from which mourning is comprised: no death notice, no obituary; mourning without a funeral; mourning with no grave. I try to clarify the murky, misleading waters, wading through the clumps of scale at the base of the memory. I make an effort to haul out the family and the home. If not in reality, then I will establish my family and their home on the written page.

Frieda lived in a small house in the town of Vandžiogala in Lithuania. Like so many families in the town, she tended a vegetable garden for the family's use, a goat wandered the yard, and every day a farmer would take the cow to pasture. The goat had her own life. Abba told me tales from before the war. About the war, the death, the guilt, the separation:

not a word. Silence. I'm now filling in those missing pieces.

Lithuania snowballed into a longing for an unknown place. The warmth, wisdom, and love harbored there were decapitated by terror and horrific loathing. Kovno, 'la Jerusalem de Lithuania'; the Jewish luminary and scholar, the pious genius from Vilnius, known as Vilna Gaon; the poets Avraham Sutzkever and Leah Goldberg; intellectuals and philosophers filled the country and so did blood, a lot of blood. I lack the shelves on which to set and drawers in which to store the events alluded to but, primarily, I am missing the tags with which to label those unnamed. As the last Lithuanian in my family, I try to melt down residues and rebuild history, weave the known into the lost, the spoken into the mute - into one entity which, perhaps, one day will be understood.

LITVAK

The Klebanovs come from Lithuania. Lithuanians are considered special, mostly in their own eyes. But they are accorded particular respect by their surroundings and are affectionately known as 'Litvaks.' Jews of all stripes - the Hassidic Jewry, their opponents the *Misnagdim*, the secular enlightenment movement known as *Haskalah* - are encompassed by the term 'Litvaks.' Overall they are known for their stubbornness, knowledge, and pedantism, dissecting every situation down to the finest details. They are illustrious for their love of strong flavors, from pickled fish to '*imberlakh*,' a piquant Lithuanian snack made with ginger. As a child, I made a concerted effort to eat herring and to hide the contortions my face made from the odd taste so that my father's friends would bestow their Yiddish praise, *zei iz tahkeh a Litvak*, 'she's a true Litvak.' Being a real Litvak was, in their eyes, the highest of compliments. Litvaks differentiate themselves from others, are often patronizing, and consider themselves classier, not only when it comes to their sharp minds and cynical humor, but also when it comes to that sharp, uniquely Lithuanian snack: hard and dry, made of carrots, nuts, orange zest and fresh ginger. Actually, that's one item I found to be delicious. Overall, everything Lithuania enchanted me.

My grandfather, Haim, was born in 1875. My grandmother Frieda, née Zilber, was born in 1880 in Taurag in western Lithuania. Frieda and Haim's oldest son, my father Yehezkel, was born in 1905 in Pajure. Four years later his sister Lena was born and, in 1910, the youngest brother Leon. The family moved from Pajure to Vandžiogala, and life was peaceful.

Zeideh Haim, Bobbeh Frieda and their three children lived in a small house. As the head Rabbi of Vandžiogala's Jewish community, Zeideh Haim taught Torah in the 'kheider,' the school dedicated to religious Jewish studies, run from his home. Some thirty-five children aged four to six learned in the kheider. Since Abba and his siblings studied with their father in their own home, the Klebanov children enjoyed the warmth of their immediate family while acquiring a rich education 'round the clock. This foundation would serve as a linchpin, fortifying them later in their convoluted paths.

Being all together and in the constant presence of their father in kheider would leave an indelible mark on the course of their lives. Although the two brothers earned their degrees far from home and allowed themselves to indulge in the company of non-Jewish women in the City of Lights, they would, in due course, abandon the charms of such temptations and establish good Jewish homes. Rarely did they mention their parents, their home, their sister. From the brothers I inherited a legacy of longing; and from their mother, the Rabbi's wife and nature lover, the inspiration for my name, meaning 'joyful.'

A TALE OF A GOAT

Today is Wednesday and the market's just opened. Frieda looks at the gray sky. Seven rays of sun penetrate a cloud, heralding a new morning. The local marketplace bustles with farmers bringing their cattle, women carting baskets laden with potatoes, the cacophony of merchants' voices ringing out from every direction possible. The air carries the musky-warm smells of animals and the sweet-sharp, enticing tang of salted fish. Herrings. Next to a booth, a farmer woman bends over her basket packed with fresh bread: black, sourdough, and caraway.

Seeing the crowd makes Frieda smile. She has no time to spare, otherwise she'd certainly go buy some black bread, tear off a big chunk and put a slab of pink herring on it, then slivers of onion and a few grains of allspice. Her stomach is rumbling, but she's come to the market to choose a milking goat. As she wanders to and fro among the throngs of shoppers, vibrant images, colors and aromas, the familiar weekly commotion lifts her spirits.

The sun comes out from behind the curtain of clouds and warms the air. Frieda removes her gloves. She's excited when she suddenly hears bleating. Several gypsies head over to the farmer but Frieda hurries to get there first. She walks up to the farmer who leads a small herd of billies, nannies and kids. She wants to position herself first in line to get first choice.

"Good morning."

"To you too. Don't I know you?"

A touch embarrassed, Frieda bows her head.

"Ah, yes, wife of the Rabbi from afterward."

"Yes. I am Frieda."

"Pleased to meet you. And what does madam wish for?"

"A good goat, one that will give me plenty of milk."

"Yes, *Rebbetzin*," he says, using the word of respect to honor her position as the Rabbi's wife, "You've come right on time. I have an excellent one for you."

As the farmer points out a white, blue-eyed goat, the animal comes over and rubs its head on Frieda's dress.

"Ah, look, she's a clever one, she is. She can see who's worth going home with."

"Indeed! Look, she's smiling at me… and what a soft coat of fur she has! Come, come, sweet thing."

Frieda strokes the goat's head. Both smile.

"But, one moment, have you not forgotten something?"

"Of course not. Don't worry."

They haggle over the price. The farmer doesn't want to lower it. He claims that the goat's produce is abundant and she is, therefore, more costly than the others. Frieda doesn't give in. She turns away as though about to leave. Eventually the farmer capitulates.

"Well, alright, may it bring us both good fortune since this is the first goat I've sold here this morning, and it's so cold out."

Frieda takes out a cotton handkerchief embroidered in blue. Rolled up inside are several banknotes.

"Have a good day, and warm regards to the Rabbi,

may he pray on behalf of us all. Here, take this rope, to be safe, and this little bell so you'll know where she is. She's a bit of a mischief, she is, wanting to run off all the time. Goodbye, farewell."

With a last stroke of the goat's head, the farmer helps Frieda tie the rope and bell gently around the animal's neck. The goat lowers its head merrily. All the way home from the market the goat trots at her heal with a, "Meh, meh, meh."

"We're almost home, sweetie. In a moment you'll meet my family. Everyone will pat you, especially little Lena. She loves animals so much. You'll meet our cow, and our turkey. Ah, how happy I am today. Yes, I can see what you're lugging about there, my poor little one, how heavy it is, it must be so tough on you. As soon as the children have gone to kheider I'll milk you."

The goat moves closer to Frieda, resting her head on Frieda's hand. Frieda strokes the little animal.

"Yes, yes, I so understand you. Don't worry."

Reaching the little house, Frieda swings the wooden gate open.

"Haim, Yehezkel, Lena, Leon, come look! Look what a pretty nanny goat I've brought home… a *tzigaleh!* Yes, yes, don't worry, my little tzigaleh, you've come to the right place!"

"Tzigaleh, tzigaleh, meh, meh, meh!" Lena laughs and sings, rubbing her forehead against the tzigaleh's nose.

And so the goat joined the family, the cow and the hyndik. A shepherd would come and take the cow to pasture in return for half the cow's milk. But the tzigaleh stayed home in the yard, milked by Frieda herself.

A HYNDIK IN THE HOUSE

Until the summer of 1941, Yehezkel was a jolly fellow, happy with his life. But from that year on, he turned reticent and rarely joked. About the war, he said not a word. When it came to telling tales and jokes, he'd been a champion, so the hyndik, tall enough to eat right from the family table, had told me. Children like to embellish tales and from each event they create, like a kaleidoscope, memories of real or imagined events, as though they'd occurred numerous times. My uncle Leon would confirm the story: its authenticity was never doubted.

The story of a turkey free to wander the house charmed me to bits. Bobbeh Frieda's compassion fanned when it came to the hyndik originally intended for slaughter. She decided to postpone the hyndik's destiny and keep him at home for a few days but, once he'd paced the yard and made the children roll with laughter, she decided he'd stay permanently and, in exceptional circumstances which became much more frequent, he was allowed into the house. The hyndik had his own life: he wandered the house as free as a king. Only in the Klebanov home did a turkey live like a family pet.

This hyndik brought joy to my father's childhood and mine.

Frieda scatters crumbs for it. "Here, take these breakfast scraps."

Hyndik pecks and brushes by Frieda's floral-patterned dress as though stroking it.

Leon asks him a question: "When's Purim?"

"Gob-gob-gob-gobble," the hyndik says. Leon rolls about laughing.

"Such a unique fellow, my hyndik. Why would we slaughter him for having never committed a crime?"

"Frieda, you're a Rebbetzin, you've earned special status, so admit it… isn't it strange? Who else lets a turkey wander around the house like that?"

"Ah, but I'm not everyone else. And this hyndik's not like all others. Right?" she asks, looking towards it.

"Gob-gob-gobble."

"See? He's done no one any harm!"

"Gob-gob-gobble."

"Festivals and morsels. Look how your protégé finds those crumbs!" Haim jokes.

"The Protégé of Vilna," Leon squeals.

"Even a blind bird can sometimes find crumbs," Frieda says.

The family had no assets. Because Haim was a Rabbi, a public servant to the community, the house they lived in was rented. Frieda and her husband Haim, the Zeideh I never had and who never had me, lived in a modest house with their three children.

I'll paint. A modest single level white house, a door without a lock, windows open to the yard. Before the war there was no 'Jude' marking pasted to the doors. I'll start with three colors. Rich brown earth. Gray skies. I'll paint the turkey in white, dot its crest in red, I'll paint the goat, adding blue to its eyes. I'll focus on shapes. After I've added the clouds, fruit trees, the vegetable and herb gardens and then paint Frieda, smiling, and smoke rising from the pots of food, will it be possible to see the house? To catch the aroma of cooking? To hear the bell tinkling?

Will Frieda stand up, wiping her hands on her apron as she does?

Will the town rise up again?

A SERMON ABOUT HYNDIK

One day, after simultaneously chuckling and wondering about Frieda's affinity toward the turkey, Haim suggested, "Come, children, today instead of a talk, I'll tell you all a story."

"Only for children?"

"No. Come, Frieda, this fable about a hyndik is for the whole family and teaches wisdom. It's by Rabbi Nachman of Breslau. A brief anecdote, and so witty. It's a story about a prince."

"Daddy, *Tateh*," Lena asked her father, "our neighbors are princes, right? The ones who live on the hill. Their daughter's a princess."

"That's right, Lena, but here we're talking about a very different type of prince. I see you're all tired, so I'll keep it short."

"Once upon a time, a prince went crazy and thought he was a hyndik and, as such, he should be sitting under the table snatching up bits of bread and bones, just like a turkey. Unclothed, of course. So that's what he did.

"Not a single doctor could find how to cure him. The king was deeply saddened, until a wise man came along. 'Let me cure him,' he said.

"The wise man undressed, sat under the table with the prince and, together, they scraped up crumbs and bones.

"The prince peered at him. 'Who are you and what are you doing here?' he asked.

"Gazing back, the wise man countered. 'Well, what are you doing here?'

"The prince answered. 'I'm a hyndik.'

"The wise man responded. 'So am I.'

"There they sat, getting used to each other. The wise man gave a sign, and a nightshirt was tossed to him. 'Do you think,' the wise man asked the prince, 'that a hyndik can't wear a nightshirt? It can indeed wear one and still be a hyndik.'

"Each donned a shirt. A little while later the wise man gave a sign, and trousers were passed to him. 'Do you think,' the wise man asked the prince again, 'that with breeches a hyndik can't be a hyndik?' So, they both pulled on a pair. And so it went, one item of clothing after the next being added.

The children listened, spellbound. Lena drew a hyndik of many different colors.

"Then the wise man signaled, and food was handed to them. 'Do you think,' the wise man asked, 'that eating good food means you stop being a hyndik? We can eat a proper meal and still be a hyndik!'

"Not long afterward, another question was asked of the prince. 'Do you think that a hyndik must stay under the table? You can be a hyndik yet sit and eat at the table!'

"And that's how the wise man cured the young prince. Clearly this story teaches us a valuable lesson."

When Haim finished reciting the tale, he added a few words. "This allegory is, of course, made up, but it actually comes from a real event and it teaches us that we don't always need to scrutinize the tiniest details of a situation to check its veracity."

"What a clever man he was," Lena said.

"With plenty of courage, and a touch of humor," added Yehezkel.

Suddenly they heard strange noises.

"What *is* that?" Leon asked.

"Sounds like a hyndik… pecking at the windowpane!" replied Yehezkel.

Suddenly the turkey peered in through the window. "Ha! Look! Here's your hyndik! Caught red-crested!"

"Very funny. He belongs to us all and you're insulting him! Especially since I do my best to treat him so nicely!" Frieda cried.

"Don't take it personally," Yehezkel laughed and gave his surprised mother a kiss on the forehead.

"Go ahead and laugh. I don't care anyway," Frieda tossed in, and smiled at her son.

FRIEDA AND THE HYNDIK

Frieda's hyndik really is extraordinary, both in appearance and behavior; and, it's true, he was much taller than average turkey, making it possible for him to eat at the table. That leaves the questions of how tall he really was and how much time he actually spent in the house. The brothers clung to the fascinating tales of the hyndik and the tzigaleh. They clung onto the past, before the war, like a colorful step-stool. Sadly, with time their innocence was lost.

As Rosh Hashanah, the Jewish new year, approached, Abba, a down-to-earth man who shunned false hope, would make the same one request. "Let it be no worse. We've already had the better."

And into that goodness - that once was, and that had passed, he immersed his memories.

I go along with the brothers' approach: on this skeleton of truth, I hang the colorful fabrication, and thus Frieda's story grows and I get to have a Bobbeh.

SHOGUN

Frieda and I share several traits: arising with the dawn, hard-working, the speed with which we hang, take down and fold laundry, a love of gardening, family-oriented, caring for animals, and a tale about a turkey.

The story takes place thousands of miles from Lithuania, in the yard of a home in Israel in a place called Ramatayim, long before the town turned into a city. This modest country house with its red- tiled roof, its family and children, its cat, dog, and little orchard, was missing a coop.

One day a friend left us an odd bequest: a brood of hens. So we built a coop in the yard, installed a solid gate, and excitedly brought the flock over: five laying hens and a lone rooster whose role had yet to be defined. The bestower of this gift advised that it was a package deal, which is why we agreed to take the rooster too. Eagerly we waited for the first round of laying, for white-shelled eggs, for the taste of dark yellow yolks. Early the next morning, after each of the family members left the house one-by-one to wherever they had to go, off I went to the coop clutching a small straw basket and feeling as though the dream of a pastoral life was coming true.

Then suddenly I noticed that the handsome big guy had taken up his position guarding the entrance and had no intention of letting me in. When I moved closer he spread a pair of formidable wings, took a few steps back as though readying for an attack on the intruder and, with lightning speed, beak pointing up, lunged in my direction, sharply nipping my jeans. Despite the denim's thickness he managed to leave a painful blue bruise.

But I wasn't giving up! Racing heartbeats and a few well-directed kicks later, I walked into the coop, found three eggs, collected them and left the fortress.

I sensed a renewed vitality. The next morning, the attack was even harsher. The guard versus me. Both of us were scared to death but both of us were ready to fight. At dawn I opened the coop's gate. This time the enemy looked even more threatening, fuming, attacked, and I was hurt again.

The next morning, I bore a weapon: a stick, which didn't help at all. The following mornings I set out for the coop holding a wooden shield, ready for physical combat with the wild assailant. Every morning my protective gear and mode of attack got more sophisticated. These morning fisticuffs were serious stuff. The pastoral vibe of living in the countryside dissolved into fear, and I was getting really fed up with the violent critter.

Nonetheless, I was not about to be defeated: these face-to-face, hand-to-wing battles taught me some good lessons. My sense of purpose strengthened. Morning after morning, when I returned from the coop, I felt a wonderful flush of victory in this survival of the fittest. Every morning I endured the onslaught and went back into the protection of our house, sighing, relieved. I'd put the basket with its eggs on the kitchen countertop as classical music played in the background, more appealing than ever. And slowly I began to realize that if not for the watchguard rooster, I'd never have achieved that sense of self-worth. It began with eradicating my fear and ended with the thrill of triumph. And so my esteem for my personal battle with the rooster grew as well as my ability to identify with him. Was he not simply trying his best to protect his territory? Would I protect my own home and my five offspring any less than he protects his five hens and their eggs?

I came to admire him: for his power, for his very being, for his tactical moves which not only reminded me of Japanese fighting roosters, but I'm sure were far smarter. Yes, my appreciation of his natural beauty and strength grew by the day.

On the mornings that followed I showed up at the coop smiling, despite being ready for our daily skirmish. Rooster made each day a challenge and, ultimately, a rewarding experience. Each morning saw a different tactic deployed. Each morning I was victorious, bringing home the prize: those fresh eggs, some still pleasantly warm. My rooster rightfully earned his affectionate nickname: Shogun. Every morning he taught me a lesson in the meaning of struggle, brawn and determination. And that's how I discovered the tough, brave rooster within me.

Little wonder that the range of non-verbal therapies I employ in my profession came to include animal-assisted therapy.

MONOLOGUE WITH A GOAT

It's so early in the morning that a silvery moon is still playing hide and seek with a pale yellow sun. Dawn spreads over the house. The door opens. With the same skillful movements she uses to braid loaves of *challah* for Shabbat, Frieda finishes the second plait of hair, feels the first with her fingertips, clutches it, holds both down with a hairpin slightly above the hairline, raises her head, and peeks at the slowly lightening sky.

Her face is smooth from the wind. Her cheekbones are broad. Her brown eyes are flecked with green. She usually only ties the kerchief to her head when she's out working in the garden. That way she protects her thick braids, which happily bob up and down on the very top of her head.

Sitting outside on a wooden chair, she removes her slippers, puts on ankle-high shoes and eagerly sets out for her garden. Everyone's still asleep. She's the first to see the heavens' colors change, to breathe the crisp air, to close the dripping tap, to hang the laundry. Every morning she goes out to check her rows of vegetables. She spies some ripe and ready for soup. As she gazes at the tree, she wonders if the fruits in the Land of Israel are juicier, more golden, but then she lets the thought drift. Busy-work leaves her no time for such contemplation.

Picking up the hoe, she turns the little garden's earth and

is greeted by the goat's first bleats. She fills a bucket with water, carries it to the goat but stops along the way, sets a stick to support a shrub that's leaned over, then serves the goat its morning meal. The goat thanks her with a nod of its head and a cheeky smile.

It's cold outside. Frieda wears a loose-fitting dress. Thick socks are visible in the space between her laced shoes and the edge of her petticoat, skimming a fraction below her dress hem. Her face is a canvas of delicate aquarelles. Her appearance is impressive, mostly because of her deeply warm brown eyes and thick brows framing them, and her high white forehead adorned in its halo of braids. Her upper body is long, fragile, reminiscent of a Modigliani figure, whereas her hips are as broad as a Henry Moore sculpture. She conveys stability, as though rooted in the earth, while her long neck seeks to rise up to meet Chagall's fiddler. Her beauty is even more pronounced by the fact that she is so unaware of it.

"Drink, drink, my sweet little one. Even when it's cold you must drink. I'll milk you soon. A little patience. These are the loveliest hours of the day, my tzigaleh, but don't tell anyone. It's wonderful when there's no prattling."

From a distance Frieda notices the farmer and the cow returning from the pasture. Wordlessly Frieda gives the farmer a bag of children's clothes.

Moving about her garden, Frieda plucks off a fading leaf, bends to pick up a rotting bit of wood, hoes, clears the berms around the trees, and again the goat bleats. Frieda sighs. She puts the light blue stool down gently next to the goat's heavy udder, shakes the cloth of her wide dress evenly across her legs, straightens her apron, lowers herself onto the stool and begins milking.

"Come, come, tzigaleh. I won't leave you to haul this around any longer. Don't worry."

"Meh. Meh."

Frieda stands, stretches and ruminates about her two sons. "You know," she tells the goat, "Yehezkel and Leon can be a bit naughty, little bandit, but they're good students and Haim is always so proud of them. They really do have sharp minds." And sits back down again.

"Meh. Meh."

"Here, look, we're finished. You're a wonderful tzigaleh. Well done. Go, go rest a little and then take a little walk. It's such a lovely day and the air is so crisp."

Haim steps outside as Frieda wipes her hands on the apron.

"What's this I hear? Talking to the tzigaleh again? Frieda, what's with you?"

"In the morning no one's around and, like children, animals love to hear stories. They listen patiently and don't criticize me. The goat gives even more milk when you talk to her."

"That's the difference between dialogue and monologue. Come, we need to eat something. It's hard to study on an empty stomach."

"Let me enjoy this beautiful nature just a moment longer, please? And can you help me carry the milk pails?"

Moments later the couple step inside.

"Ah well, I found a slice of bread. I'm going to the kheider to get the books ready."

"Haim, bread's not enough to eat, and it's stale from yesterday."

"Let it be. That'll be my morning meal for today. Anyway,

bread's a delicacy. But let me spread some of that good butter you churned on the slice. That'll be fine. At lunch we'll eat something hot."

The boys wake. Frieda prods the oven's fire, prepares food, and hurries them off to kheider.

"Leon, Tateh's waiting for you. Now's not the time to play. Don't give the hyndik your food."

"But Mama, look, he loves the omelet."

"Omelet? That's not for him. He can manage on leftovers."

"Yehezkel!" she calls, pauses, and again. "Haskel! What are you doing there?"

"Checking how much sugar goes into half a cup of tea."

"No, no, no. You and your shenanigans. What's got into you two today? We can't afford…"

"Mama, oy Mama… Leon, that's enough. Mama's right. Let's go down and learn. Today we read the Torah portion about Sarah."

"How do you know that Haskel, my little one?"

"Because that part's always read in winter, when it's really cold."

"That little devil, so smart. Sharp as ginger. I wonder what will become of him."

She pours fresh milk into a blue and gray earthenware jug and prepares it for churning. In a few days it will be butter.

HOW THE CARP BECAME A SWIMMING TEACHER

A true tale… when Lena was two years old.

Lena didn't want to bathe in the big bathtub. The water scared her. Frieda was beside herself trying to come up with a way to reassure and encourage her little girl. One day Frieda bought home a live carp, placed it in a bucket, put the children's blue bathing tub next to it, and called Lena.

"Lena! Come look who's swimming here in the water!"

Lena came at a run, gazing intently first at her mother, then at the fish. A fish swimming in the tub! How exciting.

"Mama, what a champ! He's such a strong swimmer!"

"Yes, this is a very brave fish. Lenka, come, why not hop into the blue tub. The water's warm. Quickly now, before it cools off."

While they both watched the fish, Frieda slowly, ever so slowly, peeled off Lena's garments. Lena dipped her little foot into the bathtub, gently eased in, her face startled but only for an instant, and then she squealed with joy.

"Ah! It's nice!" she said, splashing with her palm on the water's surface.

Frieda scooped warm water up in a blue metal jug decorated with a white flower and washed Lena's curls while Lena played happily in the water.

"Ah well, at last, a little girl who hasn't washed for two weeks," Frieda muttered, wiping her hands in satisfaction.

"Mama, look, he's waving with his fins. I can, too!"

Lena started making swimming movements, mimicking the fish. And that's how the carp became a swimming teacher. And Lena began asking to bathe. Two or so weeks later, Frieda wondered what to do about the fish. She wouldn't dream of killing it after it had made itself so comfortable in the bucket. But its job was over. Frieda wondered what Haim would think about the fish incident, but decided to bring the carp back to Renyeh, the fishmonger.

Taking a bag, Frieda put the carp inside, put it in a second bag so that no one would notice her peculiar actions, and went to the fish monger.

"Renyeh, hello," Frieda said softly, taking out the first bag.

"Oh! What's happened? Didn't you eat it?" Renyeh grumbled.

Frieda hadn't yet decided what words to use to explain such a contrary proposal.

"Our Lena... that is, I mean... we don't need the fish."

"What, it isn't pretty enough? Clever enough? Look, it's flesh is full and plump!"

"Yes, indeed, a lovely fish... but, how can I put it..."

"Well? And what now? No doubt you want your money back?"

"No, no. Sorry. Just take the fish, let it swim with its friends in the big pool. No, I don't want a refund. Thank you. Good day."

"Odd," Renyeh remarked, baffled. "Well, and aren't there just plenty of fish in the sea," she said, slipping the coins back into her dirty apron's pocket.

LONG-TERM MEMORY

In 1914 when Leon was four, he heard the opening shots of WWI. He didn't remember that war, and he chose to ignore the second. His family somehow coped with the first, which included moving to live in a different town.

In his Paris apartment over a glass of quality port, Leon, in a tailored suit and silk ascot, a warm smile on his face and his eyes sparkling, agrees to talk a little, cautiously, about the past. He talks like someone afraid that he might accidentally overstep the boundaries marking the area where a religious Jew is allowed to walk on Shabbat, or perhaps like one afraid to brush too close to an electric fence.

"Shoah? We don't talk about that." His family did not manage to escape from WWII, laying the two brothers the burden of dreadful guilt all their lives. It also caused them to finely hone their prewar memories. Their wartime experiences and what the war caused were not forgotten, but were met with silence.

THE LOCAL CIRCUS

The wooden gate was always shut tightly. Except for that morning. When the goat noticed it was ajar, she butted her little head against it, skipped outside, spun halfway back, and hinted to the cow that freedom is at her very hoofs. The cow, seeing the goat, followed as though saying, "Wait, wait for me, I'm coming!" When the turkey spied the two outside the gate, he was doubly thrilled, calling gob-gob-gobble louder than ever, and followed the cow and the goat.

Frieda heard the cacophony, saw the open gate, caught sight of the cow's rump just outside the gate post, and gave a rousing shout.

"Haim! Children! They've all escaped!"

"Who?... Who's escaped?... What's going on?" voices answer her.

"No time for questions! Hurry, quickly! The animals...!"

Out they ran, Lena first, then Leon and Yehezkel, Haim running after them holding his coat under one arm and his hat in the other. Frieda wiped her hands on her apron, took it off in a hurry and tossed it onto the table. She took a deep breath and rushed out.

"What a disaster! What are we going to do?"

"Mama, don't worry! We'll get them. And, if not... they'll return like *tatelech*, good little girls and boys with their tails between their legs, back to your wonderful garden. What do they think they'll find out there, anyhow? Silly-billies."

"Don't talk like that! They understand everything!" Frieda defended them.

"Come, come, come," Frieda tried cajoling. But the goat springs forward, the cow plods behind her, the hyndik leaps high and finds a resting place on the goat's back, calling gob-gob-gobble.

"Lena, look, an animal pyramid! Now all we need is for the goat to leap onto the cow's back and it'd be perfect!" Leon roars with laughter.

"What a commotion! Who left the gate open? *Nur das hat mir gefehlt*! That's the last thing I needed!" Frieda wrings her hands.

Yehezkel, the quickest of them, caught hold of the rope around the cow's neck and yelled, "Tateh, come help me! Quick! I'm losing hold!"

"Here, here, I'm coming!" Haim says as he mutters into his beard. "A real Had-Gadya story," referring to the silly song about a little goat sung at the end of the Pesach meal.

A passing wagoner watches and shouts out, "What's going on? Purim already? Need help?"

"No thanks. We'll be fine," the family calls back in chorus.

"I'll be around here for a while if you decide you need help… I just need to bring some wood to one of the scholars hereabouts," the wagoner chuckled and carried on his way.

Haim and Yehezkel slowly pulled the obstinate, heavy cow back into the yard, shouting directions at each other. The goat, startled by the shouts, stopped dead in her tracks to watch and Frieda and Lena pounced on her. Leon was running after the turkey.

"Look at him going round and round like a spinning top. What, does he think, he'll confound me?"

Leon can't stop laughing. He runs off to the side to pee, then comes back holding his tummy, doubled over with laughter.

"Hey, what fun. When is Hanukkah? Cha-cha-cha-cha, stupid bird! Do you think anyone else will take you into their home the way we do?"

At last, the four of them return to the yard huffing and puffing, dragging the cow and the goat, laughing their heads off. Frieda and Haim secure the gate and double-check it. Lena and Yehezkel go out to help Leon. Together they corner the turkey. Leon disorients it by making short sprints, first left, then right, then left again and so on, and eventually Yehezkel makes a very strange noise. The turkey stops, perplexed, turns to glance at what he thinks is the source of the sound, and bam! Yehezkel laughs.

"Bird-brain! We got you all mixed up! My trick really worked!"

Leon, standing on a tree stump, recites "Sun, stand still upon Givon and you, Moon, in the valley of Ayalon," from the Book of Joshua in an oratorial voice.

"Leonchik, that's real nice, but completely off the mark."

Yehezkel grabs the turkey by its neck, Leon by its legs, and Lena dashed ahead to open the gate. Panting and gasping, the boys bring the hyndik back, Leon's guffaws are contagious and soon his brother and sister join in.

Frieda, smiling, hugs the goat and whispers to it. "Yes, I was told you're naughty, but so naughty? What, have you no self-restraint? Running away from a place that feeds you so nicely!"

"Talking to that stupid creature again?" Haim laughs.

"Oh, she understands everything," Frieda says, retying the mussed-up bow on her apron strings.

"Well, now that the circus is over, let's get back to our meal."

"I'm not hungry anymore," says Leon, standing upside-down on his hands shouting gob-gob-gobble. Quickly Yehezkel copies him, shouting meh-meh-meh.

"A family business, this circus. Maybe Tateh will change his profession. Be a circus manager. He's so serious. Lighten up a bit!"

That night Frieda tells Haim her thoughts. "It's Boris, the Lithuanian neighbor. I'm sure he opened the gate on purpose. He was probably planning to steal my goat."

"Why would you think that… what happened? Boris isn't a bad man."

"He tries to be good, but… inside, deep inside… he's a bad man. I can feel it."

"Ah, Frieda. You and your imagination. You have silent movies running through your head."

Years later, in 1941, it would come to light that Frieda was right: regarding both Boris and the Lithuanians' attitude to their Jewish neighbors. Frieda, who had a sixth sense when it came to animals, could sense some kind of unidentifiable beast on the horizon, an extremely ravenous one, perhaps a beast of prey. But she wasn't aware of quite how massive the creature behind the thick gray clouds was growing. Sadly, her keen instincts weren't keen enough.

A GOAT PEERS IN THROUGH THE WINDOW

While Frieda worked in the yard watering the garden, Haim and the boys were just going from the kheider to the kitchen. Suddenly they heard a pipe burst. Yehezkel and Haim ran to the garden to quickly shut the tap before repairing the pipe. Lena heard the ruckus and went into the yard.

"What happened? Why is everyone wet?"

"Lenka, keep watch on the door. Make sure it doesn't blow shut."

"Don't worry, Mama, it's alright."

"Lena, the goat is scared and wants to go inside. Don't let her."

"I'm watching out," Lena said, annoyed. Suddenly she noticed the ball she'd been looking for under a bush.

"Who hid my orange ball in the yard?" Lena raised in accusation.

But no one heard. Everyone was wet and the pipe was writhing around itself as it spewed water everywhere.

"Mama, the pipe's like a snake, look!" Leon said, trying to jump above the spurting streams of water.

"Go back inside, Leonchik. All I need is for you to get sick now."

And then, suddenly, the door slammed shut.

"Lena, what did I ask? What's going on here? Where's my tzigaleh gone?"

"Look, isn't she a real queen!?" Leon roared when he saw the goat's head poking out of the window.

"Wouldn't you know - the whole family is in the garden and who's in the house? The goat!"

"Look, look," Leon yelled, "here's an odd little tale: the goat's in the house laughing at us through the window and, like idiots, we're outside! A smart tzigaleh, smarter than I thought."

"Where's the key?" Frieda asked.

"On the inside of the door," fumed Haim, "and I'm tired of this nonsense."

"Mama, don't worry, I'll wriggle in through the window," Yehezkel suggested. "Leon, c'mon, give me a leg up, and Lena, keep the window open."

Yehezkel, flexible and wiry, twisted this way and that and made his way in. A moment later his feet could be heard landing on the floor. Sticking his head out through the window next to the goat, he squealed with laughter:

"Cuckoo! You're all out there and tzigaleh and I are in here! Bye bye!"

With that, he shut the window. Haim, not happy with the whole situation, knocked on the door.

"You mischief, open up! It's Friday, Shabbat is soon approaching and the pupils will be here any moment for kheider!"

"So? Let them see our brilliant family, me and the goat in here, a soggy rest of you out there," Yehezkel chortled from the window.

Lena and Leon were howling. Frieda smiled but, at the

same time, became melancholy. The children are growing up, she was thinking, and it won't be long before they'll be leaving home, taking their nonsense with them.

Yehezkel opened the door, egging on the fun, calling out, "Come one, come all! The curtain's going up on the modern Litvak circus, and the honorable goat is walking out of the house. In a moment, the elephants and monkeys…"

And so, the goat went out, and the family went in. Two huge towels were used to wipe everyone down as they laughed, tossing gibes to each other.

"No need for the *mikveh*," Haim said, referring to the ritual bath.

"Who's going to clean up? Not me this time."

Leon, always willing to help, brought a rag and began drying the floor.

"From the way you clean this floor, we won't be able to eat off it," Frieda smiled, and cleaned up after him.

Everyone had calmed down by evening when all sat around the Shabbat table. Haim, his voice mixed with both pride and annoyance, concluded. "Only in our family could such a ludicrous thing happen."

"Ah, well, may these be our greatest troubles," Frieda answered, joining her palms together with a bashful but proud smile.

THE TALE OF THE DONKEY TURKEY

Sunday afternoon. The children are taking a short break from their studies. The turkey is wandering around the yard, it's head higher than that of three-year-old Leon. Little Leon is following the turkey, trying to imitate its walk as he yells out to it:

"Gob-gob-gobble… stop, you weird bird! Wait, wait, I want to climb on!"

But the turkey's just doing its thing, waddling and strutting around, pecking seeds and weeds. Leon turns to Yehezkel as he passes by in the yard.

"Zikki, make the turkey into a donkey for me!"

"What, little munchkin? What do you want?"

"Put me on the lyndik's back, please, just this once."

"Lyndik?"

"Hyndik…"

Yehezkel jumps up, swings Leon high above the turkey and lands him on its back, but the turkey starts running at a surprising speed before Leon can get a firm grip.

"Wait, wait, you silly bird! Leon, hold tight to the hyndik's neck!"

"I'm falling apart!"

"Into how many pieces? You're falling off, silly-billy, not apart," Yehezkel laughs.

"I'm falling!" Leon screams, almost losing his balance.

"You won't fall! Don't worry! Hold on tight to his neck, as tight as you can!"

A shout, then silence. Yehezkel can't hear a thing. He's concerned: has his brother been hurt? The hyndik keeps running, trying to shake the weight off its back. Yehezkel is muttering, worried.

"What have I done? Where are they? Probably hiding in the bushes. They're scared, both Leon and hyndik. This is not good..."

As Yehezkel starts racing about trying to find the hyndik, he hears shouts. "Giddy-up, dumb hyndik. I'm not afraid. Not at all!"

The turkey runs around in circles, jerking its body back and forth. Leon pales. Yehezkel runs to the kitchen.

"Mama, quick, give me a bone from the soup. I've got to stop them!"

"What? Stop who?" Frieda asks, dipping her fingers into the pot and pulling a bone out.

"Leon. Hyndik. No time to explain!" he breathlessly adds. Out he goes, the door slamming behind him.

When Frieda goes outside, she hears Yehezkel calling, "Gob-gob-gobble… lovely turkey, here, take the bone! Come, it's for you!"

My son is resourceful, Frieda thinks proudly, watching her firstborn deal with the situation.

The hyndik warily approaches Yehezkel.

"Yes, yes, they all think you're stupid… but, in fact…"

The hyndik moves cautiously closer, one step at a time, towards the bone.

"A better bone than this you'll never find. It's from the

Shabbat *cholent* that stewed all night. Yes, you are the smartest of them all… the turkey who lives better than any human," Yehezkel says softly.

The hyndik bows its head towards the bone. Leon's little hands are almost numb shut from gripping the turkey's neck so desperately. Yehezkel helps him loosen his fingers. Leon slides off the hyndik's back and lands like a log on the ground, breathing hard, his hands still stiff in the air as though he's still clutching an imaginary neck.

"That was lucky," he whimpers, trying to feel sensation in his fingers. Then he bursts into peals of laughter. It's contagious. Yehezkel can't help but laugh too.

"What a crazy lyndik, a real racing car!"

"Again with the lyndik? Why do you keep saying 'lyndik?'"

"Because he's a Lithuanian hyndik, isn't he?"

"Silly brother. I was worried about you for nothing."

Yehezkel stands and spreads his legs to make a tunnel. Leon zips through. They play tag. Leon tires and lies down on the grass, and Yehezkel does the same. A little while later they both roll over.

"That really was very lucky!"

"That's what happens when a naughty little boy gets it into his head to turn a turkey into a donkey."

"But all's well that ends well," Frieda whispers under her breath, watching her sons playing together. "You little bandits. Just stay healthy," she whispers, securing her braids to the crown of her head as she heads back to the kitchen with a big smile on her face.

THE AROMA OF
FRIEDA'S SAUSAINIAI

Thursday was the day Frieda usually baked *sausainiai*, crisp as wafers, and the thickness of a ginger snap "What's happened today that the batter's so thin?" she muttered to herself.

"Mama, add a bit more flour. It's dry so it will absorb the moisture in the batter and help thicken it."

"Yehezkel, how do you know that?"

"Once I did an experiment with the leftovers," Yehezkel said and disappeared from the kitchen.

"Mama, it smells… so nice," Leon announced a short while later.

Every time she kneaded dough, Leon would miraculously pop up. As she spread it with the wooden rolling pin, Leon would pull a chair up, climb onto it, nip off a bit of dough, roll it into a ball, put it on the baking tray and flatten it with his little palm.

"Mama, I came to help you."

"Sweetie, what a perfect little circle you made," she said as she continued cutting rounds with the rim of a cup. Leon puts a snippet of dough into his mouth.

"Leonchik, I don't mind if you play a bit, but be patient… don't eat fresh dough, it's not healthy."

"Remember that time, Mama, when you shaped them into all the letters of the Hebrew alphabet?"

"That was a special occasion, for first grade. Now stop nibbling. It seems tasty now but later tonight you'll have a dreadful tummy ache."

"Ah, so that's the reason why my tummy hurt last Thursday."

"Yes, little one, that's why…"

"What happens inside my tummy?"

"The dough begins to expand."

"And what happens if it gets as big as… a potato?"

"Your tummy isn't 'see-through,' little one, so we can't see what's going on in there."

"Mama, you're so clever. Wouldn't it be amazing if our tummies were see-through? Yehezkel can write that idea down in the green notebook!"

"The Great Sage of Vilna, no less! Green notebook. *Hak mir nisht keyn tschaynik*. What are you babbling on about?"

"Mama, really. He probably didn't tell you, but he has a notebook where he writes all the interesting things you say, and we also add our own ideas. Oy, my tummy hurts…"

"The samovar's still hot. Go drink some tea now to calm your tummy down."

"Do you know what else he wrote in the green notebook, Mama? Your trick, of putting dirty pots outside and letting the rain clean out the grease."

"Well, that's a fact. When it rains down hard the pots get an excellent scrub."

"You've got such great tricks. The dough I ate last week is still rising. I think it'll get as big as a melon."

"No, *sheifale*, my little lamb, the dough from last week can't get any bigger, it's long since gone from your tummy."

"That's lucky, because otherwise it might have grown and grown and then taken up all the room in my tummy and I might've blown up!"

"Funny little boy. Here, let's put this second tray into the oven."

"Mama, just one more, please, a teensy tiny one."

"They're not ready yet, Leon. The oven is roasting hot. Tomorrow, before Shabbat, you can have one as dessert. A little patience, alright?"

"You know, that's your best-smelling perfume. The aroma of sausainiai, especially the vanilla… you're the tastiest Mama there is in the whole wide world."

"Ok, time for bed, honey. Tomorrow morning we need to get up early, and you need a good night's rest."

"Wait, just a peek into the oven… to see how they rise, bursting like bubbles, as though they're chatting to each other, and getting darker… they're blushing because they're a bit shy."

"Your imagination's like a bubble. To bed now! Go!"

"Oof, all the magic happens after I go to bed. I'm not even tired!"

"You'll close your eyes and summon a special dream. For instance, about, hmmm… maybe a golden peacock. When you fall sleep it will fly over to your bed, sit on the arm of your chair, bow its crowned head, fan its magnificent tail, and show you the sparkling, beautiful colors. Every feather has a purple eye peeking out, yes, every feather has a purple eye, and so, slowly, slowly, all the eyes shut."

***

When everyone's asleep Frieda cleans up the kitchen. She cools the tray of sausainiai on a fresh towel, then slips them into a heavy, striped glass jar and shuts the lid tight, taking a whiff first. Going to the children's room, she peeks in, covers Leon, sets Lena's shoes aside so that she doesn't fall on them when she gets up in the morning, and gives a goodnight kiss to Yehezkel, whose eyes don't appear to be tightly shut yet.

"Haskel, go to sleep, what's bothering you? And she whispers, "the golden peacock… golden peacock… every feather has a purple eye and slowly, slowly, all the eyes close." She places her warm palm on his forehead. He smiles, sighs, and his eyes close.

Silently she tiptoes out and lifts her face slightly, whispering, "thank you, thank you. I ask for nothing."

YEHEZKEL MEETS A PRINCESS

Before their journey, Haim suggested that Yehezkel begin studying the rudiments of French. Not far from their home lives the Nikolayev family: respected nobility. Frieda goes to find out if one of them would be willing to teach her son French. As it turned out, their father was called to travel to St. Petersburg, so his daughter Lara was appointed as Yehezkel's private teacher.

Aside from these private lessons, Rabbi Haim and Frieda forbade the boys from having anything to do with the Nikolayev family. To Lara's and her mother's astonishment, Yehezkel caught on fast to the basics of French.

Lara looked like a real princess. Yehezkel took Leon along with him so that he wouldn't be sitting alone with her in a room. Every week Lara would lay eyes on Yehezkel.

One day she shook her blond tresses as she spoke to her mother. "Henri's going to France in two weeks' time and I barely have any more to teach him."

Henri was the secular name by which Yehezkel was known and he found this name awkward. But Leon had honed in on it and it stuck, and would continue call his brother that for as long as he was in France.

"Yes, *ma chérie*, Henri is known around these parts as a very clever student. They all," Lara's mother said in a tone of respect, referring to the orthodox Jewish community, "start learning from a very young age."

"Henri, come and listen to this. We have a record from the Red Army."

"I need to get back home to… to evening prayers," he answered and dashed off.

"Wait, just one second. I'll give you a croissant for the road. It's Larissa's own baking."

"Thank you, princess, but my mother's waiting for me. I'll eat at home. I'll have plenty of time for croissants in France."

Something pulled at his heartstrings. On his way home he gazed at the little houses, lights as orange as yolks coming from the windows. A woman hushed her three little ones, hurrying them inside, out from the cold. In the distance, a goat bleated. The aroma of chicken soup filled his nostrils. He had a keen sense of smell and could list off the ingredients in his mind: chicken, onion, carrot, potato. Stepping inside, he found the soup pot still hot. He ladled himself a bowl of soup and sat down to eat in silence, not wanting to talk to anyone.

In the evenings Yehezkel would study from the book Lara had given him, but not before studying and memorizing a section of *Gemara*. When he opened Lara's book, a delicate scent of soap filled the air. That, and the French language, enchanted him. The book came with its own fine leather bookmark stamped with the initials 'L.N.' in gold. Lara Nikolayev's personal book. Yehezkel muttered a few words in French, slipped the bookmark between the pages, placed the book carefully on the shelf, put the candle out and fell asleep.

THE BOYS' FUTURES

The sky is still gray and Frieda is already whispering her morning prayer. "*Modeh ani lefanekha*… I give thanks before You… for You have returned within me my soul with compassion…" Dawn lingers. Frieda goes out to buy bread and cheese before the children wake. Sometimes she bakes the bread herself, but today she's short on time. Wednesday is market day in town.

Back from her shopping and before she can even set her groceries on the table, the boys, who meanwhile woke up and got themselves ready, quickly pass by and grab a bite, running to kheider while shoving each other. Haim is preparing the page of Gemara he plans to teach. Lena loves being in the house with her mother when no one else is around. Sometimes she sketches the design for an embroidery she'll work on in the evening, or finely hones the 'L.K' monogram for her handkerchief until the neighbor calls from outside, "Lenka, Lenka," and takes her to spend the morning in the company of girls from the neighborhood.

Then Frieda can sip her strong black tea, and allow herself a few minutes reading "Quiet Flows the Don." She'd been fascinated by the rumors that Sholokhov had been a plagiarist. Not long ago she'd finished reading "The Death of Ivan Ilyich." Tolstoy had woven a plot where Ivan, the hero, who lived his entire life in a web of lies, never managed to rectify the situation at the end of his life. Had he been Jewish, thought Frieda, he'd have succeeded.

She learned to appreciate Gogol's sense of humor. Frieda also particularly enjoyed "The Lady with the Dog," and "Late-Blooming Flowers." She studied the logic in Chekhov's plays, such as when a gun appears in the first act, it obviously must shoot by the end of the last act! She was especially moved by the delicate weave of his short stories.

She'd heard about Leah Goldberg, her poems which touched hearts, her father who founded Lithuania's national insurance system when Lithuania was no longer part of the Russian Empire. Frieda was saddened that Leah's father had been persecuted because of his communist leanings. And she felt proud that Leah served as a teacher in the high school and became such a talented, independent young woman.

These stolen moments of reading fill Frieda with joy. She sighs, smiles, and goes back to tidying and cleaning the house with renewed energy. Going to the garden, she inspects the water and food containers, moves the garbage to the corner where she makes compost, and strokes the goat's head.

"I ask for no more than this," she says aloud by way of counting her blessings. "You know, each day is blessed. Oh, what an abrasive tongue you have," she says to the goat licking her hand, "and completely white. Tomorrow I'll give you a quality mixture, my dearest one. Don't worry, everything will be taken care of in due time. And doesn't time just escape us so quickly. The boys are already grown and the town is too small. What future would they have here? What do you think? Silly me. The answers will come with time, I believe that."

Lunchtime comes around quickly. Too quickly. Frieda prepares mashed potatoes, adds a touch of *schmaltz* and thinly sliced fried onions. Haim and the boys only have a few minutes to eat their meal and everything must be ready on time. Sometimes one of the neighbors' boys who forgot to bring lunch also joins them.

"Frieda, perhaps you should open a restaurant. It's delicious."

"That's all I need! As though I don't have enough work with the house and the yard?"

At the end of the day, when the boys have finished their kheider studies, Haim tidies the books, Frieda helps him clean the room, and then goes to the kitchen. Although they spend several hours a day apart, they are always in close proximity to one another. That night Haim comes into the kitchen.

"Oy, Frieda, Frieda, look what a mess your bird leaves."

"My mother always said that a home should be clean enough to be healthy, and dirty enough to be happy."

"Happy! No doubt about it. It's certainly happy here."

"And overall, the main thing is that my hyndik is protected here in the house. Outside it's so cold."

"What a woman I found." Haim grins. "Ah, well."

"The soup will be ready soon. It's lucky that the garden had some ripe potatoes."

Night falls quickly. The darkness and the cold expedite the children to get under their feather quilts. Quiet, at last. Haim and Frieda chat while she finishes cleaning up the kitchen and readying things for the next morning.

"Frieda, don't go to the kitchen. Why are you running away?"

"Can't you see, Haim? The soup's boiling over. I'll be back in a second."

"I've got something important to tell you."

Frieda dashes out, dashes back. "See? Here I am again."

Frieda bends easily to the floor, wiping up after the turkey.

"Out you go now, what a mess you made, you naughty bird. Look, look, the moon is a sliver tonight, like when I cut the children's nails, may they be healthy. And next to the moon, like freckles, stars in the sky."

The bird is impressed with Frieda's description and shoves the door open with its beak, stepping out. Gob-gob-gobble, it grunts, and disappears into the darkness.

Haim sighs. "Sit for a moment. You're constantly on the move."

"Here, it's all clean now. Don't be angry. *Gedult*... a bit of patience."

"I want to talk to you about something. Our Yehezkel is extremely clever, quick-witted, like mercury. Remembers every word. His mind studies everything in depth. Maybe we should let him... leave Lithuania, to go study in another country where he can get ahead. He can easily do well with higher education. I heard that France has good universities."

"France... isn't too far? How will he study in French?" Frieda asks.

"Easily," Haim answers. "He'll have no trouble learning any language. He already has Lithuanian, Russian, and Yiddish under his belt, and he's learned the basics of French from Lara. You can't imagine the head he has on his shoulders."

"That little *kepeleh*... so smart and mischievous," Frieda giggles. "But wait," she asked, becoming concerned, "will he go alone? So far away?"

"A good question, Fried'l. Maybe Leon should go with him."

"Our little lion. So far?"

"Yehezkel can help him with his studies. You see… they'll look after each other."

"Yes, maybe. Here, with all these *goyim*, Gentiles around us, I don't have a good feeling. You're right, Haim. Let's start planning."

Haim readies his fountain pen, absorbing the ink on a rounded blotter, turning it here and there, removing the excess from his palms. He draws short diagonal lines to check how well the ink is flowing, sketches a few letters in the air as though practicing, then writes a few words down on a sheet of paper, a look of satisfaction coming across his face.

"See?" says Frieda, "Everyone likes to get dirty, each in their own way. You from ink, me from soil."

"Nothing writes as beautifully as a fountain pen."

"Nor makes such a mess."

"Other than your bird…"

"Well, well."

"That talented little Yehezkel of ours. He'd be well suited to chemistry. He's always trying out impossible concoctions. With words, too."

"He stands here in the kitchen, watching, then declares: thin, thick, crisp. And he also has good hands."

"Yes. He can fix anything. A true artisan."

"His head and his hands are a blessing from Heaven."

***

In the small dye shop, Frieda waited patiently for the quality wool to be dyed. She wanted specific colors: red, blue, and white as snow. Slipping her package under her arm, she hurried home, made sure that the food was ready, sat down and, with her skilled hands, quickly knitted warm socks.

"A little more elegant. After all, it is France," she muttered to herself; a row to the right, a row to the left.

"In Paris they dress much smarter than in our small Lithuanian town."

A row to the right. One to the left. Sometimes Frieda said several words in French that she'd heard the boys saying: "*mon cherie*: my dear," and "*bien sur*: of course." She practiced them aloud repeatedly, all the while enjoying their musical sounds in rhythm to her knitting.

"I don't want his *feeselach*, his little feet to get cold."

"*Pardon*, Madame Frieda, but with whom are you speaking now, the knitting needles or the wool?"

"When I'm home on my own I find with whom to converse. When my hands are busy, my tongue waggles of its own accord."

"What an exceptional design I see there."

"*Bien sur, mon cherie*. I knitted them in France's *tricolore*."

FRIEDA SAYS GOODBY TO YEHEZKEL

"Aren't you excited? It's your first ever journey on your own, and such a long way away… from Lithuania to France. Am I perhaps more excited than you?"

"Frieda, of course he's excited but he just isn't showing it, he's already a young man."

"Mama, everything will be fine. Don't worry so much!"

"Here's the suitcase, all ready to go. I packed you lovely shirts with mother of pearl buttons, plenty of undergarments, *gatkes*, long underwear and the socks I knitted. And a surprise. Well, I'll tell you. I knitted you an angora scarf as soft as fur."

At the bottom of the suitcase Yehezkel had hidden the pair of cream-colored, knee-high socks with neat, narrow braids on either side which Lara had knitted for him.

***

Frieda fusses around her son, not knowing whether to sob or smile. Yehezkel grips the handsome leather suitcase, an old one that the Nikolayev family gave him in honor of his trip. He surreptitiously lowers his eyes and runs his fingers gently over the letters, the initials embossed along the side of the suitcase: L.N. Lara Nikolayev.

***

My father, Yehezkel, first left Lithuania in 1927 with the goal of gathering information on study options and preparing the ground for his, and his younger brother Leon's, move there.

The difficulties at the outset foretold the complexities they would experience further on. Yehezkel was like two people in one: serious, but amusing; scientific yet mischievous; a man but still a youth. He was like fruit that had ripened too quickly. The modest leather suitcase in hand, he traveled to learn of the application process and entrance requirements of the university. Deep in his pocket was his brand-new passport, leather bound. Passports for Jews at the time were few and far in number. It was a travel permit showing 'Nationality - Lithuanian; Religion - Jewish.'

The Lithuanian passport bore Yehezkel's surname with the typical Lithuanian suffix: Klebanovas. For the first time in his life, he was exiting Lithuania. His passport number was 58. Only 57 passports had been issued prior to his; at that time, so few were traveling about the world.

Apprehensive yet determined, Yehezkel stayed in a small hotel in Paris. From there he traveled to Lyon, and then to Perpignan. At each university he presented his younger brother as someone who was also befit for higher education. Their years in the kheider had keenly honed their minds. And so, Yehezkel described his studies there and was warmly received by the Deacon in his chambers.

THE BROTHERS IN FRANCE

The moment of farewell arrived.

Their high school studies completed, Yehezkel and Leon went to study in France, leaving behind, forever as it would ultimately come to be, their home, their parents and their sister Lena.

Their places assured, Yehezkel returned to collect his younger brother. But Yehezkel received a letter which required his earlier return to sit for an examination. Leon arrived in France later, in 1930. They both lived in Toulouse, but each studied at a different university. Yehezkel studied chemical engineering and was already a second-year student; Leon was studying electrical engineering and so, Yehezkel helped Leon with his studies. Their closeness and interdependency grew strong.

Years passed.

***

"France," Frieda whispers. "Paris... I've never been there. Tolstoy wrote about it. So did Turgenev and Chekhov. Everything there is *comme il faut*, with a certain etiquette. The women sip red wine, smoke slim cigarettes, wear high-heeled shoes, very revealing silk tops, and walk *engagé*, arm-in-arm with young men…"

Wiping her hands on her apron, she glances at the reflection of her faded house dress in the mirror, tidies up some wisps of hair, and smiles. Haim is watching her.

"Frieda, your cheeks are pink. You just blushed."

"I was thinking about the streets of Paris. Those slim Parisienne women, so busy with their hairdos and their fancy clothes. Things we're never concerned with."

"Charm is deceptive, and beauty does not last, so says the book of Proverbs."

"I saw a magazine with shiny photos. The women were elegant, beautiful."

"You are beautiful also on the inside, without all their silly trimmings, a trait that will last for years to come."

"With such hard work, who knows how long it will last," Frieda sighs, "how much longer I will last."

"*Hak mir nisht keyn tschaynik*! You're befuddling your own mind with all that nonsense."

Frieda and Haim would joke about who'll die first, who'll come to whose funeral, and what will be engraved on the headstone. They do that because they believe that it will bring them many more years of happiness together.

HEALTHY PREMONITIONS

Missing his family a great deal, Yehezkel came for a home visit in 1934. And, as one who loved pulling pranks, he didn't give them any prior notice of his arrival.

Seated in the train, Yehezkel was gripped by excitement as the landscape shifted from France to Lithuania. In another hour he'd be in Vandžiogala, alighting, heading for home and surprising his family, especially his mother.

In the small house, without understanding why, Frieda was on *shpilkes*, restless and anxious.

"Frieda, what are you dress up so nicely for?"

"Do I have to wear the apron all day every day?"

"Of course not. But what's got into you? You're different today."

"Haim, I'm so excited."

"For what?"

"I wish I knew. But my stomach is in knots. Perhaps…"

"Sit a moment. You've gone pale."

"Maybe Yehezkel will come? Today? To visit?"

"What? What are you talking about? Did someone tell you that?"

"No. But I feel it."

"Ah well. She feels it."

"It's time… I'll be off to the train station now."

"Impossible, you can't go. It's terribly cold out and you aren't even sure…"

"But I know. I do."

"Oy, can anyone argue with you? I need to teach now, otherwise I'd walk with you."

"I'll go slowly. There's time. I feel it. I made you food. It's all ready."

"The house is so spic and span. What an effort you made! Did you even rest for a second?"

Frieda doesn't answer. She leaves the house, her right palm over her pounding heart. She walks to its beat and whispers to it. "Shhh, calm down, easy now, there's time yet for leaping out of my chest. Today, time is unimportant. Shhh…"

In the distance she hears the train's horn howling like a jackal.

***

Yehezkel's stomach was also queasy with excitement about the surprise he had planned for his family. Surely Mama will be thrilled. And Lara? No, he wouldn't go to her. He removes his beret, fluffs his curls, scratches his scalp. He doesn't need anything from Lara. He speaks French fluently now like a Frenchman. In fact, he could teach Lara plenty. His association with her caused his father grief. He's now so engrossed in his studies, distractions won't do him any good. His studies are precious to him but require a good deal of attention. He needs to save his strength, work at the building site in the mornings, and find time to tutor his brother. Yes, he needs to stay focused.

He's exhilarated to be visiting his hometown. The plan is, he'll go his house, wait a moment for his heart to stop racing, knock at the door as though it's the neighbor bringing wood for the stove.

To the click-clack of the train's wheels over the sleepers, he dreams up tales and ideas, some of which he jotted down in the green notebook, its cover now creased. He's been travelling for hours, allowing him time to closely assess the differences between the French and the Lithuanians, between the warmth of Yiddish, his native tongue, which has the taste of hearty chicken soup, its plethora of jokes that are simultaneously sad and happy, and French, the language of love.

So far he'd busied himself with equations, with Mendeleev's periodic table, with test tubes, pipettes, and filters, Petrie dishes used to examine the color produced by burning zinc. As a scientist, he was well aware of the secret of combinations. As a chemist, he understood the secret of combining the real with the imaginary, the spiritual with the material, and knew that for a compound to succeed, it needed air, wind and a reaction.

Dressed as a Frenchman in a long, tailored coat, beret angled on his head, he stepped off the train. No one would be waiting for him, nor would he wait for anyone.

Vandžiogala's single railway track is relatively dark compared to the massive grand station at Gare de Lyon. Only a few people quickly move across the platform, not wasting their time. In France people sit languidly in coffee shoppes sipping *café au lait* or *citron pressé*, which is basically lemonade. Being French means striding to your destination with a baguette clutched under your arm after taking bites of a croissant slathered with butter and blueberry confiture, then resting a while before setting out for an art exhibition. But here, in Vandžiogala, the hands of time are set a century back. Unlike in France, the Lithuanian that guards the small lone train platform marches back and forth, armed with his weapon.

What's this? The figure of a woman standing alone on the platform, immobile as a statue. Perhaps she needs help, or is waiting for someone whose arrival was delayed. Her hands are grasped together inside a fur muff. Who could she be waiting for?

The clothing is familiar, but that couldn't be. After all, he didn't give notice of his arrival. Dressed nicely, her back a bit hunched, admittedly, but the gesture of her head speaks of nobility. She fixes her gaze on him but does not approach. She still can't believe it.

"Mama?"

"Yes, yes, my son!"

"What are you doing here? How did you know?"

"I knew! I just knew!" Frieda starts to whimper. "As if your mother wouldn't know!? I also felt it when you fell ill a month ago, and knew you had a high temperature."

"Yes, that's true, but I didn't write to you about that."

"A pity to waste good paper and ink on that. A real mother feels it… inside… in her gut, not in her head."

The stress that had been building up lately suddenly burst under the pressure into a flood of tears. Yehezkel had been making such an effort with his studies, at his job, helping Leon. Frieda had been sensing a strange tension in the air for a while now. They stood embracing for several long minutes.

Laborers stepped up onto the train and began cleaning it. Excited travelers waited on the platform. When the trainmaster's whistle sounded, people began taking their places in the carriages. Those not traveling remained on the platform, waving farewell. A young woman cried out to deaf ears. "If we don't meet again…" a man's voice carried with the wind.

Hooting, the train's horn sounded, blocking out all the rest and making it impossible to hear. As it rolled out of the station, Frieda lightly caressed her son's cheek.

"Come, let's walk home, this cold will freeze our bones and Lena has made you a surprise."

The guard, who'd been approaching them, suddenly turned and went back.

Arm in arm, *engagé*, they walked home. No one could have imagined that this would be Yehezkel's last trip home.

COINCIDENCES

Coincidences have always fascinated the human mind. A thought that travels 7,000 kilometers from Hod Hasharon in Israel to Machu Picchu, Peru and feels what a loved one is going through. The angle of the sun finds a tiny lens in the forest, ruins and realities that the intellect cannot fathom let alone explain, especially their timing. People who share intense empathy reading each other's thoughts. This enigmatic sense of foreboding is what brought Frieda to meet her firstborn at the train station, though neither had any inkling this would be their last encounter.

LENA RECEIVED NOTHING

After presenting his parents with gifts from France, Yehezkel called his sister over.

"Lena, come here a sec..."

"I see you brought gifts only for Mama and Tateh," she said.

"Oy, my sweet sister, let me explain something."

"Haskel, I was teasing you. I already have everything I need."

"But I want to tell you a secret. I saw a gorgeous brooch, handmade, and I'm saving up. Very soon I'll be able to buy it for you. It's made of pure silver filigree, with branches, flowers, and two people. It's such a beautiful picture and it reminds me of us, you and me, when we were little and playing together, as if..."

"As if what? What are you dreaming of?"

Suddenly Frieda calls out from the kitchen. "The *latkes* are hot, come, quickly," she says as the waft of freshly fried potato fritters fills their nostrils. Frieda wipes her hands on her apron.

"Where's everyone?"

"Yes, coming," Yehezkel answers. But unlike the way they all used to rush to the table, this time everything seems to be happening in slow motion, as though stepping gingerly between sorrow and a wish to take advantage of every moment at home, postponing for just a few more moments the pleasure of Mama's hot latkes in favor of sitting and chatting together quietly for a little longer.

THE SEAL

The silver brooch eventually became mine: delicate handiwork that my father purchased for his sister with the hope that one day he'd be able to gift it to her. When, years of despair later, it became apparent that he'd never be able to, he gave it to me. It felt like a flame in my hand. I couldn't bring myself to wear it, as though the pain sealed in it would leave a burn mark. Warmth and deep love are embedded in the brooch, as is an ocean of nostalgia. These emotions are what give the piece its value, making it more of a keepsake, a memorial.

A silver, round brooch like this, handcrafted in such intricate detail, can no longer be found. On it are flowers and two figures. The one on the left is a woman carrying two buckets; on the right a man carries a staff. I've just lifted it out from the safe and polished it to remove years of tarnish accumulated from non-use.

Long before I was born I'd already lost a family, a home, and precious treasures. Sadly, I seem to have an innate tendency to set things down and forget where I put them and then, only when I discover the loss, do I feel the weight of my carelessness. But it's not so much the object I've misplaced as what was lost many years earlier. That's why I found it so difficult to wear the silver brooch my father bought for Lena. I didn't believe I could wear it. I was afraid: wearing it came with an inherent fear of losing it. Another loss.

Now, I place my right hand over it, pinned to my blouse above my heart, and feel its filigree; this brooch, meant for Lena, my aunt, embosses my heart, leaving an impression. Only now, seventy years after my aunt's death, am I able to wear it. A commemoration of Lena in perpetuity. A small consolation. A minuscule victory. An effort to null the annulled. I peer down at it, seeing it upside-down, and now I understand why the elderly have trouble seeing up close. I cannot make out its details from the lapel of my blouse, but I can if I look at it from a greater distance, from the perspective of family history, seventy years earlier.

Two miniature envelopes lie in a rusty tobacco box. Their edges are tinged with rust. Each envelope is marked in clear handwriting: the relevant year for the photographs inside. Some from 1927, show young lads in the body-covering swimwear of the time. Another shows Yehezkel, age twenty-two. The second envelope, marked 1935, must be from Lena's visit to Lyon when Yehezkel was thirty. Lena is a slim young woman of twenty-eight. The photos are hard to decipher: like the Dead Sea Scrolls, snippets of words need to be fleshed out and, from these few photos, the story slowly takes shape. Expectation is in the air, much like children who join the numbered dots to finally display the picture.

Yehezkel's brief stay in Lithuania filled him with joy and sorrow. He changed a broken roof tile, laughed with his mother in the kitchen, hopped over to visit a friend in Kovno, bought vegetables in the market, swam in the river and, suddenly, the allotted time had run out.

On the same platform where he'd met his mother a short while earlier, Yehezkel said goodbye to his parents and sister, his neighbors and acquaintances, still not knowing that this departure would be forever.

A STRANGE DREAM

One morning Frieda woke upset. "Haim, you hear? I had a very strange dream."

"Ah, my wife, forget about dreams. You won't go far on a dream. As it is, our reality is so complicated."

"Deciphering dreams has become very fashionable of late. I read that they are allusions to reality."

"As though we don't have enough to learn from Torah, Talmud, history, languages! Should we now let dreams bother us too?"

"Haim, sometimes, whether you agree or not, sometimes the soul wants to speak, and it has no words. Its language is dreams."

"Ah well, I'll clean my fountain pen and sharpen some pencils and you, if you wish, can tell me about it while I work, and that way I won't waste my valuable time."

"I dreamt that I went to the shoemaker to fix a pair of shoes. I asked Lena to bring them back from him. The little one went and brought back a bag. I open it, and what do my eyes see?"

"A demon? A monster?"

"Enough already, be serious."

"How can I be? You've turned the day into night. Nothing will come of this"

"So you continue with what you're doing and I won't tell you."

"Ok, ok, I'll be as quiet as a wall. Tell me, what did your pretty eyes see?"

"I see a pair of shoes, but both of them are for left feet."

"And does that mean something to you?" Haim makes an effort to connect to his wife's frame of mind.

"Don't they always say, 'start out on the right foot in order to succeed?' But here were two left shoes, which I couldn't wear, and couldn't walk in, as though there's no way to 'start out.'"

"Ah, great… as though you didn't have enough to worry about, now this dream is going to worry you?"

"Not really. I just wanted to tell you about it."

A DREAM ABOUT A PARTRIDGE AND A MAGNIFICENTLY WINGED BIRD

Frieda gives up trying to interpret her dreams. When she goes out and tends the garden, they unravel on their own. Thoughts come to the surface like a grain suddenly spied by the hyndik, popping up and revealing themselves when the time is right. Since these are Frieda's dreams, let's put them aside for now. Perhaps they'll clarify one day, like her butter.

A TINY HOLE CALLED 'MEANWHILE'

'Meanwhile,' one word indicating a duo, bridging between this and that, a suspended state. It's a vital word in the kitchen and in life. There's no reason to rush. Meanwhile, while the oven is warming up, we can get organized.

It's a pivotal term. Meanwhile - the oven heats. Meanwhile - we don the apron. Meanwhile - we arrange the ingredients, the kitchen utensils we'll need: bowls, spoons, the chopping board, the knife, meanwhile.

Frieda's mind whirls with thoughts, thoughts she's hankering to share with Haim, but go unsaid. "Where shall we go? We have no possessions. We can't sail to America, nor to Israel. Perhaps the dreadful decrees will be held back. Perhaps they'll evaporate. Meanwhile, all's well. Don't worry, everything will work out in the end. After all, don't you talk to God, consult with God, appeal to Him? I'm not at all sure you get better answers than those I get when I talk to my tzigaleh, but at least she answers with an audible 'meh, meh' - sometimes."

Meanwhile is a word that undermines the validity of the constant and emphasizes the temporary and transient. Sometimes we want to ask a loved one, "Will things be alright? Will they be as they always were? It won't get worse, right? Promise me?"

But coincidence and the provisional are the victors. 'Der mentsch trakht, un Gott lakht,' the Yiddish saying goes: a person plans, and God laughs. Even those who enjoy the best of lives may suffer. Like a bag of sugar we decanter into a jar but, from a tiny hole which we never noticed on the packet's other side, half spills to the floor, and look, the kitchen, which was sparkling clean moments earlier, is messy again. Sweet turns into bitter. Suddenly water drips from the tiniest pinhole in the bag carrying the goldfish we just bought and the little fish, who never did anything bad to anyone, is dying and can't be saved.

How many of us have such tiny pinholes in our souls from which the good every so gradually seeps out and, over the years, the bad slowly creeps in. Our facial features begin to droop. Someone tosses out a sentence that makes us realize we aren't as good as we used to be or would want to be.

Sometimes we discover a fault on the boundary between good and bad when a close friend doesn't speak the truth, turning everything on its head, and we ache with the pain of separation. It's easy to overlook or dismiss the impact of the drip-drip-drip of toxic venom building up and bubbling inside; and people just carry on, going about their day, putting up a front as though nothing at all has changed. Only come Pesach we all sit around a seder table asking, '*Ma nishtana*,' what has changed? The questions hang in the air and even the wisest cannot provide answers.

For some, evil permeates their insides, not for a visit but takes up permanent residency, causing harm to everyone and everything in their wake.

'Meanwhile' - the naïve hope that evil is temporary and, given time, will turn to good, at least for a while. However, 'hope' is already the good bit, and waiting offers only temporary consolation.

Meanwhile, the men, women and children of the Jewish community, ever-hopeful, ever-faithful, believing 'everything will turn out for the best,' waited for the good… and disappeared.

CHANGES TO THE BROADCASTING SCHEDULE

Sometimes Abba would sigh and say, "The Diaspora is so pretty." What a paradoxical combination. Not 'Lithuania' or 'France,' but 'the Diaspora' is what he was pining for.

Before going to sleep I snuggle into a quilt of longing, soft and white. Longing for the unknown, for something else. Not for something, not even for a specific person, but for that which cannot be expressed in words. Yearning for a different life. A hazy hunger for Russian steppes; for a home with an address I don't know; for music… Red Army songs. For French music: Edith Piaf, Yves Montand, Jacques Brel, *Frère Jacques*, *compagnons de la chanson*, poems by Jacques Prévert. Sometimes, for flamenco. Guideposts Abba left in countries and along winding paths he traveled from Lithuania to France to Spain and, eventually, to Israel. Longing for Bobbeh Frieda to hug me, sing a melancholy Russian lullaby, perhaps a song about a lark.

A song about a lark that won't disturb soldiers taking a respite from the war's horrors. "Slavie, slavie, nitrevoje te soldat." Catch it, catch it, don't you disturb the soldier. We Interrupt Your Regularly Scheduled Programming to Bring You This Breaking News: then ending has been changed, the producer decided to rewrite the final scene. Suddenly the curtain goes up and there's Mickey Mouse smiling away, saying "juuuuust kidding." A lovely grandmother, in her lovely apron, calling me when the latkes are lovely and warm and ready to eat. Welcoming me, her granddaughter, just as I am. And telling me, as she was once told and as she told her sons, "*Zorg zikh nisht.*" Don't worry.

NOSTALGIA AND COLLECTIONS

Memories I placed in the drawer developed in the incubator's darkness.

I had a hobby. "Raising traumas." I settled them into white cotton-wool.

I placed them in the light and watched how these tiny things develop, send out gray arms,

searing. In the evenings I sorted the traumas: the darlings, they all developed nicely

and unnoticed, took over my fig tree and my grapevine.

At last I decided to place them between the pages of books, slowly drawing the air out of them,

And that's how I began a new hobby: "Parching traumas."

Longing is a sensation closely linked to the terms 'nostalgia' and 'days of old.' Boxes. Containers. A collection of writing tools, papers, fountain pens, an irrepressible need to document, to reconstruct the timeline, to leave a mark. Hanging laundry in the sun; stroking an animal; milking the goat; fixing an old object, patching an old garment; hand-stitching a doll. Going back in time. Not getting bogged in idle chatter. Reading poetry. Delving into literature, into sources. Enjoying a fascinating quotation.

Hearing about a new book, like one in dire need of a dose of caffeine when their shift is over, running to the bookstore like a junkie seeking the dealer. Enthusing over an insight as though it's a satisfying soup warming the heart. Astounded and filled with wonder by the fruits manual labor.

Years after your death, Bobbeh Frieda, I feel true longing. If I knew the truth of what really was going on in your life, I wouldn't be telling your story and anecdotes about your yard and animals each time in a different way. This current endeavor of mine serves occasionally as prayer or meditation, and sometimes leaves my hands lost. I feel like an ant carrying a large load on its back and, despite my limbs crying out, the ligaments wearing from the burden, I continue, doggedly persisting in bearing the true past which I do not know, and its imaginary parts which are already intertwined. And like a braid of highlighted strands of hair, not knowing which are the original colors and which have been tinted at the salon, such are my feelings about your past, which is mine as well.

Instead of all the collections, I'd like to collect you and bring you to my home, sit you down next to me, listen to the story, ever so slowly, from your own mouth. We'll sweeten tea with cubes of sugar held between our teeth as my father, your firstborn, suggested. That way the flavor is never the same; the amount of sugar in each sip of hot tea is different. What fun is it stirring in the sugar into a uniform taste that leaves no surprises? We'll sweeten our conversation with tangy jam and bread, we'll hug and be silent together. Silence. After all, the spoken word is a perforated bucket from which experiences flow.

MUSE

It happens every so often: I am visited by the muse, who suggests I expound now and then, walking her two fingers between the lines, saying "yes, a bit more here, and here." I watch those fingers perusing up and down the rows of text, and between the lines it sends me a message. "Come, come, some filler here, and here."

I spoke to the muse. "But I don't know anything about Lithuania or Bobbeh Frieda beyond what I've written."

"Then be inventive." responded the muse.

My imagination begins to soar and the words start rising to the surface and come out in a steady flow.

This discovery brings me tremendous joy, an almost existential happiness, but also brings choked-back tears to the fore. I don't cry, I just yearn. The longer I spin these yarns, the more I feel they are the truth. The muse revels in my happiness and is saddened by my sorrow.

And so, I answer. "It's okay. I know how to be quiet. Today, for example, I was quiet with Bobbeh Frieda. So let's be still together, all three of us. You, me and Bobbeh Frieda."

"You mean all four of us," proposes the muse, smiling, because she's already inextricably interwoven within the story. "You, me, Bobbeh Frieda and tzigaleh."

In just a few minutes we'll hurry off to our regular

activities. But until then there's time, and we can be comfortably silent together. We're in no rush."

Fascinating occurrences arise as I write. Life finds its way into the story and the past jumps forward into the present. Dreams turn out to be reality, and vice versa. When I'm with the muse, Frieda begins talking and then, a short while later - and you won't believe this, but - the family turkey wishes to be heard.

Muse breaches the heavens, listens silently, encourages; but does not absent herself once she's given. On the contrary. Her transparent wings are part of the cycle of nature which never ceases, continues to surprise, as lightning might. I find this unusual connection invaluable. Imagination and reality interlink, the manuscript thickens, and the muse accompanies it all the while.

"Tuesdays are Muse Days." We set up a snippet of measured time, quality time, and yet so transient. Transience heightens and empowers the sense of fullness and enjoyment.

This interaction bolsters and motivates me to continue, to carve, to write.

EMERGENCY PENCIL

The writing process brings pain to the surface. As much as I was aware of this phenomenon, I hadn't fathomed its power. Together with the pain, leafing trees grow from within me; wreaths of purple flowers. It's like Shiatsu, where pressing on painful points makes contact with sources of chi, allowing the energy to flow freely through the channels and rousing the body for acceptance of such strength. As such, the words heal as they hurt.

Depending on nutrition and atmosphere, the body self-heals, becomes a repository of its own remedies and antidotes. Writing is an infinite fountain of the finite. Writing is vitality, a life force. It is the answer to death's finality. Death is a given, life is not. Every line is a matryoshka, a nesting doll, leading to the next. A story begets a story. The fabricated begets reality. Reality begets the imaginary. Writing lies awake until I reach the last matryoshka, the smallest of all, which cannot be pried open.

That last little matryoshka, not meant to be detached, can be cracked opened by the power of words.

THE SHOAH MATRYOSHKA

Shoah matryoshkas are surprising; their exterior is different from the interior. When you open her up and reveal what is inside of her, and she seems to be familiar, inside her another doll opens, a wise one, a terrible one, a happy one, an apathetic one, one who is generous and, inside her, one that's wicked. The next doll that opens is usually very intelligent, reads literature in several languages, Freud, Heine, speaks logically and, suddenly, a small, blunt, disturbing matryoshka comes out of her - the smallest of all, the innermost one and, try as you may, it is stubbornly remains closed.

Holocaust survivors are like human matryoshkas. Outwardly they seem completely fine, organized, efficient, and sometimes pleasant, even enchanting; but pry her open and you may find that the one beneath is a stinging, evil witch. Under her is a sad one; and under her, is one that tells the other to stop complaining, but she herself cries non-stop; and beneath her is a frightened one, and inside her the courageous one, then one strong as an ox, and the next is weak, her fire has been extinguished like a little birdie that's lost its wings; and last of all, last but not least, the tiniest, teensiest one - blue, pure, like a teardrop.

Here's a matryoshka I was shocked to discover in the therapy room:

At a family event a cute young fella, the son of the lass's friend, sat on his mother's lap. The lass was also dreaming about a little boy who'd one day sit on her lap, but they weren't married yet and she wasn't mature enough to be a mother. Suddenly, as she sat comfortably on the grass, a strange thought came to her mind. She didn't see the thought as cruel: she would take a knife and kill the little boy.

This lass, who was thinking about the murder of her friend's boy, is the granddaughter of a Shoah survivor.

SECOND PERSON

Frieda, do you know how strange this is? Did you know that I had a second grandmother, my mother's mother who died around the time of my bat-mitzvah? Nevertheless, it is you I long for; you, who was never a grandmother to me and is no longer with us. There's no designated plot to stand by and ponder, to shed a tear, to place a small pebble. Yet something in me blends into you, into your non-beingness. The reflection of that what lacks any tangible existence exposes the parts that wish to be drawn into existence, pleading to be painted, in more lines and in an ever growing array of vibrant colors.

The faded photos left behind of the home you lived in and of our family cry out to me from some forgotten drawer, somewhere, in a drawer I've yet to find. Yet, I still I don't want to find the box, if the box even exists, containing a photo or two of you and my Zeideh, Haim. So strange and painful: I never used the word 'Zeideh' for Haim until I was forty-plus. Suddenly, as a grandmother myself now, I can connect to you, my dear departed Bobbeh who I never saw. I won't raise you from the grave, but I can give you a life between the pages that have been ripped out.

Here you are, hovering like a spirit above my computer, this new-fangled writing implement you couldn't possibly fathom. You couldn't have imagined that, one day, you'd have an eynikl, a grandchild, who's sitting here for hours writing about you on this wonder-machine.

And at once, you we are fused. I sketch out your memory in bright colors. Because, back then, everything was blacker than black, gray, the rare sprinkling of white which struggled to break through the bleakness. I succeed, 'just like back then,' to retouch the black and white photo with colors: blue skies, red lips, rosy cheeks, and presto! it's as though the photo has come to life.

But how is it possible to color a white page with no photo? Therefore, I'll have to start from the beginning, from scratch. To snap a photo in my mind of the house, of the kheider, of all the members of the family, the garden, the goat, the cow, the turkey, and then, with those sketched out in gray on the page, I can color them in with pastel shades. I stare at it and sigh. Perhaps a cloud will slowly lower itself, pale blue, and I'll stop rummaging in the past. Perhaps it was this way, or some other. I poke at the ground like a hesitant archeologist who has no idea where the dig begins or where it ends. Beseeching to breathe life into the dead.

The Lithuanian Jews, who loved to study Torah, had a bevy of phrases that included the Yiddish word *shtikaleh*. A little piece. Yes, much like in German *stück*. *A shtickaleh broit*: a chunk of bread, or a piece of herring, or a stub of a pencil, a scrap of paper: a *shtickaleh papier*. Writing instruments are vital. My emergency pencil is manifested from the nib of their pencil and a slip of paper, and the thrill of learning, writing, documenting.

The war trapped them in various countries: while the boys were studying in France, the parents and sister remained behind in Lithuania in the tranquil town. Frieda was saddened by her boys' absence but understood that they had no future in the town. At home, all was as it ever had been; the hyndik continued prancing about and, in the yard, the cow and goat munching as they wandered to and fro. The animals became Frieda's friends. She found it easy to talk to them and they, unlike others, let alone God, always took her at her word and at least responded aloud.

FROM A JOURNEY SEEKING ROOTS TO A JOURNEY OF LEAVES

July 2009. I planned to fly to Lithuania, the land where my forefathers were born, and visit the graves of my paternal Bobbeh, Zeideh and aunt. I prepared a ceramic tile on which I'd inscribed each family members' name, and intended to place it on the mass grave where my family was buried. I wanted to see and feel how they lived in faraway Lithuania. The search for my roots became a recurring motif. It's hard for a tree without roots to thrive, and it can easily deteriorate.

By the time I renewed my passport the travel group had filled up. I cleared my calendar for ten days, marking them in my diary as 'Lithuania.' When a new group opened up I was very happy and the first to sign up, but it turned out there weren't enough registrants and trip to Lithuania was canceled. And it was clear: that summer I wouldn't be going.

I wanted to tune the knobs in my mind's transistor radio to a happier station, to break loose from Lithuania's jaws. So retreated to the north. A gift to the body. I viewed it as a sign. I registered for a wellness workshop, to be alone, to change something. And so, I came to Amirim, a lush, organic agricultural community, and set my suitcase down at its gate. I noticed a woman in a headscarf and a man with white hair and was taken aback, concerned about the group composition. A whole week requires quiet, and so I waived the toxic thought. Let the quiet commence.

Five o'clock in the morning, white drifts of fog caress the mountains overlooking the Kinneret, the Sea of Galilee. A dream I remembered awakened an idea. When hiding, the door needs to be left open because the person chasing us is looking for a locked door; and when the pursuer comes across an open door, he'll pass right by the one who is lying low.

At five AM the universe is still drowsy and quiet envelopes the mountains. Like Bobbeh Frieda who cleaned her garden at dawn, I did too. I need to work the earth, remove stones, uproot wild weeds from the garden inside me.

Timing is the king of coincidence. As the invitation stated, there would be a talk-circle in the evening where each participant will share their story. Rahel, who I met at the entrance, tells that she was born in Lithuania. That evening she removed the headscarf, ashamed of her manner of dress. In her childhood, in order to save her, her father sent her to hide with a non-Jewish neighbor. There she stayed hidden for a long time. At three years old, her mother finally found her. To this day Rahel knows nothing of her family. She is weighted by sorrow and cannot find a way to heal herself.

For a week I tasted the atmosphere of Lithuania. The journey to my roots alternately exposed hatred and pain, and uncertainty doesn't always make room for knowledge.

Another workshop participant spoke of a fascinating book he'd read: a math lecturer in the USA takes revenge for his family murdered in Lithuania. Not far from the lecturer lives the man who, by chronological order, murdered his family: first the littlest children as their parents watched, then the parents as the grandparents watched, and lastly the grandparents. The book's protagonist decides to avenge the murders. He produces and edits a film about the murderer's children and then entraps the murderer, imprisons him in a room, and shows him the film about his seemingly murdered children. It causes the murderer dire sorrow. Leveraging the man's emotional state, the protagonist proposes that the Nazi murderer write a suicide note, presents him with cyanide, and suggests he swallow the pill. In the court case following this event, the judge has difficulty determining if this was a case of a murderer who murdered a murderer, or a suicide.

Is the tale fictitious? Is the plot about daring, a sense of mission, a journey of revenge? The murderers of my family have remained abstract. I prefer to focus on the love I have for my family rather than dig into the Yad Vashem Holocaust Center Archive in Jerusalem with the aim of exposing the murderers' identities. I fear that more questions will just open their mouths. I don't feel revenge.

During the workshop, Rahel talks about the horrors of her childhood in Lithuania. Following her second visit there and hearing the rest of her family's story, she came back ill. Three Jews hidden in the village were discovered by the Germans and killed on the spot. A neighbor turned informer: she provided information about a fourth Jew hiding. With the help of this neighbor and several well-trained dogs, the Jewish man was found. It was Rahel's father. He was interrogated to disclose his daughter's hiding place. Not a word left her father's mouth - not as they tortured him, nor when they broke his hands, nor when they plucked out his eyes. That is how he saved his daughter, as well as the family that hid her.

Rahel's mother returned to the town when the war was over. She noticed a little girl having trouble with exposure to sunlight. She presumed it was her daughter, the girl who the farmer's wife had hidden for years in a sack. With the threat of war always nearby, and in the absence of the father, meeting the daughter was a sorrowful event. Fruma, Rahel's mother, found out the name of the woman who informed on her husband's hideout. She decided to take revenge. Fruma gave a Lithuanian farmer a bottle of vodka as payment for locating and eradicating the neighbor who turned Fruma's husband over to the Nazis. The farmer went off into the forest with the woman, and came back some time later alone.

Rahel passed away some time ago, but her story has not been forgotten.

***

Although my first trip to Lithuania had been cancelled, Lithuanian-ness brushes by me wherever I am.

In April 2010 I did travel there. For six months after my return from Lithuania I was unable to write a word. Over the years, the sorrow at the unnecessary deaths of my family became dusted in a fine layer of limescale, the kind that sticks and is hard to remove. Nonetheless, this one-sided endeavor to become closer to my Lithuanian family was underway, powered by the accumulating question marks. Insight doesn't always grant precise answers.

***

Dawn breaks. It's 6:00 AM. The sky is a heavenly painting, a cerise and mauve mingling with blue and white, a streak of colors too magnificent to name. The earth, which does not wish to be aroused from its slumber, is slowly revealed, begging to sleep a while more, still swaddled in a blanket of clouds. A silvery moon concealed by the overcast eventually comes to life, sloughing off its gray cloak. A page in an artist's sketch pad cannot replicate the beauty. With a good rinse, all the colors are easily removed and the page is white again, a clean slate; the humidity transforms the vivid colors into pastels with a warm welcome, starting afresh: forgetting the past?

Like Bobbeh Frieda, I don't wish for more than that.

***

Amirim has replaced Lithuania. Instead of going back to my roots in Lithuania, I chose to breathe fresh mountain air. But the search continues between the pages. My desire to get closer to Frieda, to understand what transpired in her past, carries on. I add imaginary chairs around the dining table and fill each seat with a family member's spirit. The past is woven with the present, and brought back to life. In my mind's chessboard, where life and death switch places, the game of life and death is dependent on the written word. Like in a Klimt painting, on the dance floor made of white paper, generations dance, generations of the dead and the living. As with Op Art, optical illusions trick the eye of the viewer; all that is in the distance comes closer and that which is in the forefront withdraws and slips into the background.

SAFETY PIN

*A window frame faces the vista, studies a hummingbird
hovering above a roof, linking house and sky.
A door connects a family to the earth, in the doorway
a mother is patching clothes, safety pin in hand,
restoring all that is torn.
The eye of the needle glances from side to side and, in the
patchwork quilt, a man seems to be curled up, an old man.
The nib of a pencil seeks to write a poem but instead must
list the shopping: bread, milk, corn patties for the little girl,
and don't forget matches.
And between the Shabbat Shalom and Happy Holidays,
time trickles, snails carry their homes, the girl has
become a woman and she too has a roof protecting from
the occasional downpour.
Windows, wide-eyed, gaze towards the neighbors' homes,
and mother dozes on and off ironing creases, looking off into
the horizon where faded houses bear red roofs.*

FEAR

I once heard that it's possible to detect cancer patients by a common trait: they become increasingly fearful. My father never drove; perhaps he feared driving. In my childhood we ordered taxis for longer drives. When he fell ill, he became wary of registered mail showing up in the mailbox, a gratuitous fear income tax forms. After my mother passed away, my father married his neighbor, Batya, also Lithuanian. In light of what happened to his family, especially his father the Rabbi who had such deep faith, my father decided to abandon all religious practice whereas, secular Batya, a Holocaust survivor, swore that if she were saved, she'd become religious.

When he fell ill, Batya was his devoted caretaker. One day she asked me to help her hang laundry. As I started, she came over and quietly leaned in towards me as though sharing a secret.

"Hang the pajamas and underwear on the second row," she suggested. "The neighbors don't need to know that there's a sick person living her."

Both feared; both knew how to hide things.

The fear wasn't new. It began with the Nazi beast, somewhere in the thickets of Lithuania.

A TRIP BETWEEN THE CLOUDS

A cloud's life is brief. Memory is rebuilt like strips of cloud forming into one larger one. I never met Bobbeh Frieda but, were she at my side, I'd take her for a walk through the streets of Tel Aviv and take her for a stroll around the paths of Hod Hasharon. I'd hold her warm, bony hand and show her the land that she'd never seen before. The place where Jews live in relative tranquility. Calmly, proudly, I'd lead her through the streets and show her a new world, one she'd never been privileged to see.

I'd feel the longing fade, the loneliness waft away, whereupon so would the fear.

GUT FEELINGS

Despite the cloud of concern, or perhaps because of it, the community was more cohesive than ever, unified by the joy of praying together at top volume in the synagogue. Children came to learn at the kheider. Gardens grew vegetables. Animals grazed. In the kitchens, women continued cooking and baking. Fairs were run as usual. Wednesday markets filled with new items, caraway bread, black bread, bright orange ginger, wheels of hard cheese, an abundance of fruit and vegetables, sophisticated tableware, graters and tureens, top quality pots and pans. Now and then there were some whispers among the Lithuanian farmers but, for the most part, everyone was polite and friendly. Frieda's gut feelings mislead her. Only a handful of Jews decided to leave the town.

In 1940, while her sons were studying in France, Frieda spent much less time cooking and, more and more, she'd stand, lean against the sink, wipe her hands repeatedly on her apron and stare blankly. She didn't know whether or not to share her concerns with Haim. On days like these she loved baking sausainiai. Fridays she baked braided challah. When she had her plans for the day all thought out, she felt protected.

Since Lena ate very little, every so often Frieda would pack a small amount of cooked food for a neighbor's ill child. Stepping outside, she sensed something in the air had changed. She no longer ambled at a leisurely pace, but hurried to bring the package to its destination, her head bowed, finding it hard to contain what she felt only wanting to return to her safe home as fast as possible.

"Haim, it's good that the boys are there. What's going on in France now? No letters have come for quite a while. What do you think?" she asked hesitantly.

The grandfather clock ticked loudly. Frieda watched the timepiece swing from side to side and was reminded of the gypsy woman who gave her a pendulum. Frieda still used it, although only rarely. It had been a very significant gift. Sometimes when Frieda was worried she'd use the pendulum, but only when she was alone as she never felt a need to share this with anyone.

THE SEER

After an event which Frieda foresaw had indeed come to pass, a neighbor popped in to consult with her. Slowly, neighbor after neighbor would pay her a visit to ask her advice about a remedy for a child, a quarrel with a husband, a long trip. Over time the circle of people knocking at Frieda's door expanded.

At times, when she had no response, she would go the corner of the room to the small wooden table, open a hidden drawer, and take out a silk sachet tied with a red ribbon. She never told anyone about the trinket as she didn't want Haim or Yehezkel mocking her. On those rare occasions when a neighbor was anxious about her or a family member's fate, she would open the sachet and take out the pendulum: crystal, transparent, hung on a fine silver chain with a ring at the end.

She'd clutch the ring in her fingertips, take a few deep breaths, then address a question to the pendulum. "How would you manifest a positive answer?" And the pendulum would swing back and forth from Frieda's bosom. Then she'd put another question to it. "How would you express a negative answer?" and the pendulum would swing from side to side, left, right, left, right. Then Frieda would draw in a long deep breath. "And now, please, answer this for me," and present a question regarding this one's health, that one's journey.

Only when absolutely necessary, when her gut feelings didn't seem to be responding well, Frieda used the pendulum for herself. "Is it good for the boys to go to France?" was one of the questions she asked, and the pendulum answered in the affirmative, swinging to and from her bosom. With trepidation, she asked, "Is Yanek a good match for Lena?" and felt uneasy about how she'd worded it. "Yes," came the response, and Frieda relaxed.

But when it came to one particularly fateful question, she had no idea how to word it to ensure a yes or no response, so she waited patiently for the perfect moment. One day Lena came rushing into the room and Frieda, who was holding the pendulum right at that moment, quickly hid it in her apron pocket.

Lena stopped short. "What were you holding just then?"

"Just something trivial."

"Mama… didn't you always tell me that the smaller the object, the more precious it is? So what is it?"

"It's, um… how can I put this… my secret consultant."

"Come on, be serious…"

"Yes, Lena, I am being serious."

So Frieda told Lena the story about the crystal pendulum hanging from its delicate chain with a ring at its end.

"Oh, Mama, seriously?"

"Yes, my darling girl."

"And Tateh? Does he know about this?"

"Mmmm… no."

"In that case, I won't tell him either. But now I want to ask a question," Lena said in a hush.

"If you make fun of this, I won't let you try."

"I'm not making fun, I'm curious. Mama, please," Lena begged.

"Here, hold the ring with your fingertips for a while, feel it. And in your heart of hearts, ask a question."

"What kind of question can I ask?" pondered Lena.

"Only you know, and the question should be one of importance. Don't trouble the pendulum with silly things."

"I have a question, I think. How should I ask it?"

"While you're reflecting on the subject, ask the pendulum what a positive answer would look like."

Delicately, Lena held up the ring in front of her. The pendulum began to move. Lena's face became serious.

"Oh, sure," Lena laughed suddenly, "because I'm moving it to get the answer I want."

"Well, I could see from the start that you didn't believe in it. Here, give it to me, sweetie. You can try some other time."

"No. I'm sorry, Mama. Let me try once more."

"What would a positive answer look like?" Lena asked the pendulum.

Suddenly the pendulum moved back and forth.

"I don't believe it!" Lena gasped. "It works!"

"Show me... what would a negative answer look like?"

The pendulum began to swing side to side. Lena stared at her mother in wonder.

Frieda nodded, smiling. "Now you are ready to ask your real question."

Lena bowed her head. A crease showed on her forehead. "Will Yanek be healthy?"

The pendulum moved neither back and forth, nor side to side, but swung in circles. Lena's eyes questioned her mother.

Frieda whispered. "Lenka, ask again, using a different wording."

Lena thought for a moment. "Will Yanek and I... stay together?"

Holding the pendulum reverently, she watched. "Yes," it answered.

Lena gave a cry of joy. "Oh, how wonderful! Mama, thank you, thank you so much!" and she ran off to her room, relieved.

Frieda feels a sharp pain in her stomach. Something about the second answer, unlike th-5
e first, bothers her. The door slams shut. Frieda is alone in the room once more. She fears asking the pendulum again so just whispers to it, "Thank you."

She rubs the crystal's edges to a shine, then slips it back into its silk sachet. "Now rest," she whispers, "there will be more questions to come." Some days go by and Frieda is beside herself: how can she find a way to properly ask the pendulum again? She finds herself suddenly phrasing a question similar to that of Lena. First she asks only in her mind, soundlessly. Then she whispers.

"Will we all stay together?"

But because she immediately thought of Yehezkel and Leon in France, she rewords the question.

"Will Haim, Lena and I stay together?" The pendulum moves slowly in circles but then stabilizes into a positive response. Even though Frieda is still not fully reassured, she whispers to it, "Thank you." She wipes it lovingly on her white dress sleeve until it sparkles, returns it to its small holder and, as gingerly as if cupping a newly hatched bird, places it back in the drawer

One morning Lena came running to Frieda, out of breath, and threw her arms around her mother. Frieda took a step back but instantly relaxed, returning the embrace. Frieda looked at Lena, her eyebrows raised questioningly. For a while now Lena had been more distanced from her mother, her behavior even a bit insolent, but Frieda chose to remain silent. Frieda experienced the this as rejection and was saddened by it. She remembered when Lena was a little girl and would hug her, seeking her advice. Lately they were becoming more like strangers.

"Mama, Mama, give me the pendulum... I have to ask," she paused, "a very disturbing question."

Frieda smiled. "But only if it's a very serious matter." Lena nodded vigorously.

"What does your positive answer look like?" Lena asked. The pendulum moved forward and back. "And what does your negative answer look like?" The pendulum swung from side to side, left, right, and again.

Emulating her mother, Lena took a few deep breaths and slowly whispered her question. "No," the pendulum responded very clearly. Lena followed the very strong side to side movements and became distraught.

"Mama, where did you get this pendulum from?"

"Ah, leave it, Lena, it's a long story."

"Mama, some things are worth talking about now because who knows what tomorrow might bring."

"Alright, Lena, but just don't look at me with those sad, sad eyes."

"What can I do, Mama? There are things I just can't hide from you."

"Years ago," Frieda began, "do you remember when I

bought our tzigaleh in the market?"

Lena nodded and her expression softened. She looked just like a little girl excitedly anticipating her bedtime story.

"My sweet daughter, that's better. Well, I met a gypsy in the market. She wore brightly colored clothes and stood next to one of the goats. I went over to pat the goat. The woman came up close, smiled, and asked me a question. 'Madam, why are you so worried?' I was taken aback. Yes, I'd been through a tough time, but I couldn't understand how she'd know that. Usually I never talk to strangers about anything but this time… how should I put it… a small door opened in my heart. 'You're right,' I said, 'things aren't easy right now.'

"She felt about for something. I sensed that I needed to ask her a question. 'I hear you have ways of solving dilemmas?' The woman nodded. 'If you're interested, come sit with me in the corner.' She had kind eyes. I had no idea what she was referring to, but I was drawn to her so I followed. We sat on a tree stump. She wore a dress and a headscarf, so many bright colors, and she gave off a faint odor of goat's milk. 'Madam, worrying doesn't help. Our people have a very simple item that helps us. Here. A pendulum.' She drew this little bag from her pocket. 'You can ask it one question. It makes life easier,' she smiled at me."

"Mama, weren't you scared?"

"No, Lena. I felt that we had a special connection… a sisterhood. And also, well, you know me. I was very curious."

"So the gypsy pulled a small crystal from a red silk sachet. She explained what to do, just as I explained to you. I asked my question. I can't remember now what it was, but I just remember receiving an answer that allayed my fears.

I held my hand out to shake hers, thanked her, and told her that she just saved me. With her warm, coarse palm she gently stroked my cheek and suddenly said, 'It's for you,' and placed the pendulum in my hands.

"We sat a little while longer and she explained a few details about when and how to use it. To this day I can't understand how such an odd thing can help. But I've found it to be very calming."

Rapt, Lena gazed at her mother. "So every time you have doubts about something, you use it?"

"Only rarely… and I always keep the kind gypsy in mind when I do."

Frieda fell into deep thought as she wiped the crystal until it shone. She put it back in its silk sachet and never opened it again. Times had changed.

WHAT THE FUTURE HOLDS

Frieda knew when to feed the children, when the first raindrop would fall, when a rainbow would appear high in the sky, when to bring the goat water, when to hoe the garden, when Shifra would give birth, when the farmer would come to take the cow to pasture. But Frieda, who knew a thing or two about life, was unable to predict what the future held. Even her finely tuned senses could never have foreseen the Holocaust.

The evil was to become a monster of such scope than it was beyond nightmares. A massive beast, its head splitting into a thousand heads, similar to the modern-day children's toy, a *Bakugan* which, when placed on a magnet, writhes and swells into a different creature.

When the residents were ordered to leave their homes and climb up onto the wagons, Frieda packed some warm clothes, obeying only because she had no other option. Before leaving the house she hugged the goat and whispered, unclear whether to the goat or to herself.

"Yes, I've left you a pile of greens in the corner, in the usual place. Well now, here's our big hyndik. What are you up to?! Very funny. Standing on the fence making strange sounds. So different from your usual ones. Are you hinting at something? Do you also sense something in the air? Perhaps you can tell me what it is? You, who always dined at our table, who knows us so well. What is this? It's good that Yehezkel and Leon aren't here. Haskel would surely be able to explain these upsetting circumstances. And Leon? He'd give that half-smile of his. Such a good, sweet lad. So naïve, he probably wouldn't be bothered by it.

"Yes, yes, I'm coming!" she calls in answer to the others urging her on. "Did I lock the door? What does that matter? And the key? What does that matter? What's gotten into me! How is that important now? Yes, I'm coming. Goodbye, house. Goodbye, warm home. Goodbye, cow. Goodbye, our funny bird. Goodbye, my little white goat. Goodbye farmer, if I don't come back, be sure to take care of them all… no, don't promise… who knows what will be?!

"I have a bad feeling. I can't explain it. Something huge which I can't comprehend. A severe threat. Gray clouds are scudding along in the sky and there's not a drop of rain. Trees are brown, and tired, bare of fruit. White homes frozen in place, bare of people. A strange wailing, not of a baby, it's deeper.

"I can't explain it to you. It's gigantic, unlike anything I have ever seen. I have a bad feeling. But Haim and Lena have already gotten onto the wagon and I'm joining them now. No, don't be sad. No, it's not you. It's my tear, dropping onto your eyes. I don't know if we'll meet again, or when, or how."

The hyndik rested his head on her apron.

Frieda gazes at him and, in her mind, an image surfaces.

LULLABY

Frieda could never have imagined that the war would eradicate all that she'd built. As much as hope does console, it can also mislead. The town's Jews were ordered to gather in the synagogue. What were they thinking as they collected their belongings and locked their homes? Did Frieda realize that she'd never return? Never again see the garden, the house, the goat, the turkey?

Wooden wagons cart crowded neighbors. Someone sobs. Some hush whoever it is. The rest are silent. A terrible silence. What is there to do? We're going. That's it.

It's cold. Everyone is huddled together as if embracing, as if asking: What is this? What is this absurdity? The horses don't understand the change in their usual route either, it's a new path. People jump off as quickly as they can, grabbing their possessions, pushing and shoving and hurrying into the synagogue. Who can imagine what they were thinking, feeling inside that synagogue as they waited for the unknown?

A soldier at the entrance rebukes them.

"Go, go on! There's no time. I've got other jobs to do today."

Frieda whispers, "What kind of work does such a young fellow have to do? Why is he so angry? Or is he worried?

Everyone sits, crowding together. All chairs in the tiny synagogue are occupied. The young people sit on the cold floor. Frieda takes out a thin blanket from her tote and passes it to Lena.

"Sit, my little one. Sit."

"Why are we here? What are we waiting for?"

"I have no idea," answers Frieda but, to herself, she saying, 'waiting for something, something.'

Haim strokes his beard and leans in close to Frieda, whispering. "Fried'l, what are you thinking? What's this new crease furrowed between your eyes?"

"Something's unclear. It can't be."

"What can't be?"

"What I'm thinking."

"It's *gurnisht*. Stop worrying, Frieda. Worrying doesn't help. Things will work out. We have to believe. Like always. What can possibly happen? The main thing is that we're together." But his words don't even console himself.

"That's exactly the thing. This time I don't know, I have no… Good that the boys aren't here."

Haim's worried. His wife usually predicts rain. How many pupils will come to study. When the fair will be held. Which of the two, Yanek or Peter, will be Lena's fiancée. On which day of the week the neighbor will give birth. And if it will be a boy or a girl. She can predict the day and hour with precision. When the bulbs will sprout. When the lark will appear. And now, of all times, when these forecasts are needed the most, her power of prognostication isn't working. Something's gone wrong.

The synagogue doors suddenly slam shut.

"No one dare try leaving!" the soldier shouts. "If you do, you won't return!"

A little boy bursts into sobs. His mother hushes him.

And herself. "Shhh, shhh."

Fatigue and fear fill the thick air. Some fall asleep. Someone sings a lullaby. A child laughs loudly. Night falls at a snail's pace, like the eyes of dead man refusing to shut. Ever so slowly, the gray turns deep black.

"No stars," Frieda whispers to Haim. "The halo around the moon is strange. There are actually two halos. Did you see? One light, and one has a strange reddish hue. I'm sure it means something. I have never seen such a phenomenon."

Days go by.

The Jews are imprisoned in the tightly shut synagogue.

The soldiers stand at attention outside the front door. Someone outside whistles a sad song. *"Slavie, slavie, nitrevoje te soldat. Pousti saldati, nimnoje paspyat."* Catch it, catch it, don't you disturb the soldier; let the soldier sleep a short while.

"Who are we waiting for?" children ask. Parents try improvising answers. "For whom are we waiting?" the adults ask.

For two solid weeks the Jews remained cooped in the synagogue. Their clothes stink of sweat. The corners of the room reek of urine. Food is getting scarce. Those who feel hopeful about being rescued encourage those who feel despair. The deafening silence is broken by the soldier's whistling. On one occasion, when no one noticed, he dragged a tub of water inside.

Suddenly the doors are violently kicked in. Noise, shock, a blinding light. The soldier who kicked it is shoved inside, head bowed, the tip of his nose brushing the tips of his black boots. In his wake come seven Lithuanian soldiers talking among themselves and looking as if they were on a serious mission. Haim, understanding every word, muttered to himself:

"It couldn't be!"

Lena screeched. "It's not possible! We didn't do a thing!"

Lena was the first to be shot.

Haim grips his only daughter's hand. Slowly, slowly, her hand's warmth dissipates. Frieda clutches Haim's hand and senses Lena's lifeblood leaving her. With all her strength she presses his hand. It returns a little warmth.

"Whoever speaks will be shot. You saw that brave woman, yes?"

The soldiers load their guns. One chuckles.

"Well, it won't be difficult for us this time. They're hardly moving. And there's no escape from this place."

"Those girls who put up a fight made our work tougher. Only after shooting them in the legs did they finally go quietly, hopping on one leg like ducks. And then we buried them alive. They had some nerve!"

"Shut up! Shut your traps, Nazis!" a tall young man shouted, his mother trying to silence him.

"We're Lithuanians! We're much more methodical and cruel than Nazis!" the amused soldier answered in a blood chilling scream.

"Stand up, fella! What exactly did you wanna say? Can you repeat it?"

As soon as he opened his mouth to talk, a round of bullets blasts him.

"Ha! So you're not repeating it? We get it. Apparently, the fella changed his mind," the soldier mocked, turning to his mates.

The moment of death.

Shots pierce the silence in the synagogue in the small town of Babtai. Silence. Screams. Some words of prayer. And then, as one, they collapse.

A red silence.

***

The Holocaust is a massive stain; it is fire, it is frost, it is emptiness, it is a monster, it is a catastrophic cataclysm caused by one man and a handful of helpers. I'm far too inadequate to paint the Shoah, the town, the synagogue, the death, the silence, the mass graves.

I see Chagall's paintings: a boy rides a turkey. A couple is in heaven. A fiddler is on the roof. I can see in Samuel Bak's paintings where the landscapes are boulders engraved like headstones. I can see in Yosl Bergner's painting, the 'Flying Grinder' where grates are like clouds in the sky. I could, like my father, photograph, paint, write. I could embroider, concoct, bake sausainiai with Frieda, watch them rise in the oven, comforting and curing the family of any and all ailments, all before that August summer day in the year nineteen hundred and forty-one.

***

Rabbi Haim Klebanovas was the Vandžiogala Jewish community's last Rabbi. He was murdered by the Lithuanians on 5 Elul 5701 (28 August 1941) following a two-week detainment in the Babtai Synagogue along with his wife, Frieda, their daughter, Lena, and hundreds more Jews.

The Register of Communities, Lithuania

I learned of this horrific event only in the year 2000. For seventy years Abba and my uncle Leon held onto the hope that their sister might have escaped, but she did not. The fact that my grandfather's name is listed is of little consolation. What remains of Zeideh Haim, Bobbeh Frieda and my aunt Lena is not just Testimonial No. 19345 held in Jerusalem's Yad Vashem Holocaust Memorial Center, but a film which is always screening in the private movie theater of my mind. Nothing was left of their past other than a few black-and-white photos. And me, to fill in the gaps.

WOUNDED

Death is painful to those left behind. And there is suffering even more painful than death. If they'd only shot and killed them, they'd have done them a mercy. You know the paralyzing photo of the boy who raises his hands in surrender that appears in books about the Lithuanian Jewish community. But what you won't see, due to their lack of modesty and its cruelty, are photos of the young Jewish women ordered to remove their clothes, march naked, their bodies healthy, supple, in their peak of blossoming, their skin soft, their stomachs flat, their breasts firm.

These young women bore the ultimate humiliation. The Lithuanian kareivis, outfitted in his decorated uniform, stood behind them, his gun ready, playing cat and mouse with them. His aim was not to shoot them in the heart, a quick death, but first to maim them. He shot at their legs, crippling them. And there they were, naked as the day they were born, unable to react or to flee. His goal was utter humiliation. The young women were exposed, floundering.

Anyone who couldn't walk was considered dead.

Marching with perfect posture and confidence discloses a person's character. A limp causes deformity of the body as a whole; it is a source of insult, mockery and ridicule for a cruel heart. Here these young women are, darting around between the Lithuanians' bullets, limping towards the pit. In another minute they will feel earth tossed onto their long, flowing hair, onto their bodies which have yet to experience love.

Instead of a kiss, their mouths will taste clods of bitter earth.

I didn't see the pit. It's long since grassed over but, from a distance, I hear the shortness of breath, the rustle of clumps of earth, the satanic laughter of Lithuanian soldiers.

Frieda never said a word to me but if, let's say, my Bobbeh had spoken to me, it would have sounded something like this: "*en men hot nisht in kop, hot men in di fis.*" Literally translated, 'when you have nothing in the head, you have it in the feet.' In other words, plan ahead. It is a saying that acts as a warning to one who forgets something and has to go back and run around looking for it.

No need of a photo. The image in the mind is enough to be heartbreaking.

WAR FOLLOWS THE BOYS

Before WWII broke out, Yehezkel and Leon left behind their carefree childhood and their loving, close-knit family to seek a better life outside of Lithuania, unaware that they would soon be the family's sole survivors. In 1927 they were accepted into two different universities. With determination and great effort, the brothers studied in a language completely foreign to them, worked morning jobs to pay their expenses and successfully completed their education. Each graduated with a degree in engineering, then deemed the elite of degrees. As qualified engineers, both were able to earn comfortable incomes. On September 29th, 1930, Abba received his diploma from Toulouse University, however, he had still not received any information regarding his family's fate.

The motion picture running through my mind goes from classic film noir to technicolor, from a silent movie to a 'talkie,' with sound. Sounds of silence and screams. It changes from a children's movie like 'Heidi the girl from the Swiss Alps' to a horror film shown in 3D. I blow life into Bobbeh Frieda, expending all the oxygen in my lungs, completely draining me and leaving me breathless.

Might she have expected both her boys to survive and go on with their lives? Bobbeh Frieda, who in the days of war couldn't comprehend the madness playing out in the vicinity of the Kovno province, in her little town of Vandžiogala a stone's throw from her green garden, her white goat, her turkey, would surely have known from her place in heaven that both were spared, and would have smiled.

Might she have whispered, seconds before the gun was drawn to face her soft brown eyes, "Thank God Haskel and Leonchik aren't here."

Was she sad that the God she believed in had disappointed her? In those last moments, did faith become meaningless as she witnessed the entire community obliterated before her very eyes?

Yet God hadn't entirely disappointed. There were still some scraps left. After all, the family had a past as well as a present, the present being written at this very moment for the sake of the future. The two orphaned brothers supported each other all throughout their lives, as close as a pair of twins. When Abba fell sick he never said a word to us, his children. He told only his wife and brother.

But at this point in my story, the brothers had not yet known about their family. The following period was a stormy one - Spain's civil war broke out in 1936 and ended in 1938. WWII broke out in 1939, the year Germany invaded Poland.

A year later, France was conquered by Germany. The war seemed to be tracing the brothers' footsteps.

PITCHFORK

The brothers are in France. They have no peace. The Vichy government passes laws against Jews. The Law of 4 October 1940 gave discretionary power to detain and imprison all Jewish foreign nationals. Left with no other option, Jews were on the run once again, already having been forced out of their homeland, from France to Spain. Every refugee tried her or his luck in one way or another.

In 1943 the brothers fled southern France for Spain via the Pyrenees, the mountain range straddling the border of the two countries.

"How will we pass the border?" Leon asks.

"Don't worry, little brother."

"But I *am* worried. And we've heard nothing from Mama and Tateh. Not even from Lena. Letters used to get through, despite being stamped with a swastika. But since that last one, not even a postcard. She wrote in Yiddish, *mama lushen*, so that the oppressors wouldn't understand and, since then, nothing. Why are you so quiet?"

"Because you haven't stopped talking. Don't worry. Don't think about the family right now. We've got to concentrate on crossing the border."

Yehezkel looks around and sees a wagon carrying hay. In fluent French, he talks to the farmer.

"We... both... want to cross the border."

"Why should I care?"

"Allow us to join you just until the border, some three kilometers from here."

"My horses are weak, as you see."

"We're skinny. They won't feel us at all."

"Oh, they'll feel you. Of course they will."

Leon begins to cough nervously, choking back tears. He doesn't want to give his older brother something more to be concerned about.

"Please. I'm scared," Leon says softly.

"Don't start begging. It won't help," Yehezkel speaks to Leon in Lithuanian. "Talk to me in Lithuanian."

Turning to the farmer, he switches back to perfect French and, with a decisive tone says, "50 Francs. Not a centime more!"

"*Merci. Merci. S'il vous plait.* Climb on, both of you. Where are you from?"

Whispering in Russian, Yehezkel warns Leon. "Say nothing or they'll be on to us, the whole deal will go down the drain."

They climb on, sinking into the soft hay.

Slowly, but surely, the horses walked right across the border between France and Spain.

"Wait! Halt!"

"What is it? What do you want?" the farmer addresses the guard in broken Spanish.

"All kinds of bandits are coming through lately, fleeing to Spain."

"I go through here every week. You know me."

"Not you and not your mother! Today I'm going to check thoroughly. I don't believe anyone anymore!"

***

The guard picks up a pitchfork, raises it high, brings it down forcefully into the hay, raises it again and brings it down, and again, and again. Just inches from their ears, the brothers heard the swoosh of the pitchfork and the shouts of the border guards.

"For sure someone's in there. Those filthy *Zhyds*… surely they're hiding here!"

"No, no, it's the stinking frogs who want to infiltrate the border!"

"Try again in the middle! Push it in hard! Deep!"

Clinging to each other, the brothers shake in fear. "We're finished," they whisper. "Oh, Mama," Leon whimpers silently.

The guard gives a shout to the farmer, "Alright. Go on now!"

"Giddy-up!" the farmer commands his horses and clicks with his tongue to encourage them. As the horses gain speed, their rhythmic trot rocks the wagon and calms the shaking brothers. Destiny, having been so cruel until then, was gracious this time.

"God surely loves you," the farmer shouts once they gain some distance.

"Some kind of love," Leon bursts into tears.

Jumping down from the wagon, Yehezkel flicks snippets of hay off Leon's hair, closes his shirt's top button and tightens the scarf around his neck a little. Leon does the same for his older brother, doing his best to hold his tears back.

Winter is particularly cold in Spain that year. The brothers start walking, slowly at first, then a little faster. Not far from the border they've just crossed is another one with even more guards. The two cross at Portbou, in Catalonia, northeastern Spain. This time they're both caught, accused of trespassing, and taken to the Gerona Jail south of Barcelona.

"I don't have the strength to continue," murmurs Leon.

"Hold on, my brother. We've gone through so much. A little bit more. Remember what Mama always told us: Patience, have patience."

For nine months of 1942 the brothers were imprisoned. How information carried in those days is hard to know, but the fact is that the news reached its destination and saved the brothers' lives. They needed to prove that they had relatives in the US, and money was sent to them from America in a brown envelope.

The Cooper family of Baltimore not only proved to the brothers that they did have family, but even donated a sizable sum, enough to bribe the prison guards. I don't know who he was, but an engineer named Svetia helped secure their release in 1943. Abba held onto that brown envelope until his dying day.

Released from prison on a cold wintry day, having been stripped of their family, their home, and their country, the two orphans set sail on the 'Nyassa' for the port of Haifa, arriving in Eretz Israel in 1944.

SAILING TO PALESTINA, SOON THE LAND OF ISRAEL

The war formally over, institutions immediately focused their attention to the "Second Wave Immigration" program (with assistance from the British Units in Israel who had been sent to help the British army in Europe), to rescue Jewish children, most of them orphans who had just been liberated from concentration camps or who had found refuge in Christian homes, institutions, etc. Even before the Second Wave activities were underway, pressure was exerted on the American, French and even British Allies to allow these children legal entry into what would shortly become known as the State of Israel, while simultaneously reassigning ships designated to return discharged soldiers to their countries of origin for this humanitarian mission. It is not known whether the British allowed this wave of immigration by issuing special certificates of entry, or whether the immigrant count was deducted from the allotted 1,500 monthly entry permits the British were issuing as part of their policy to prevent large-scale immigration of Jews to the British Mandate, but some of those liberated from transit camps were balanced against the preset quotas.

The 'Nyassa' set sail from Spain to Haifa with WWII refugee immigrants early in February 1944.

From online information about the refugee immigrants' sea journeys.

The Joint Distribution Committee, commonly known simply as 'The Joint' or JDC, helped release the Jewish captives from the Gerona prison and send them, via Portugal, to Israel. At the time, the term 'quota' set the number of persons designated to be saved. On 22 January 1944, the Nyassa set out from England via Spain and carried some 800 Jewish refugees, among them the brothers Yehezkel and Leon, as well as several French Jewish intellectuals, including their close friend, pharmacist Dr. Bella. Nyassa was the first immigrant vessel to receive a sailing permit. The sense of comradeship among the survivors helped them start new lives in their new-old home country.

THE FATE THAT LINKED TWO BROTHERS SEPARATED THEM

Could Frieda have imagined that it would come to pass that her two sons would not only survive, but immigrate to Israel, arrive at Kibbutz Givat Brenner not far from the Weizmann Institute in Rehovot, meet up with several other Jews from Lithuania (among them one of Lena's closest friends), drink fresh carrot juice, walk carefree in citrus orchards, have their photos taken in Old Jaffa, see the blinding light of the Holy Land, feel the sun's warm rays on their cheeks, visit the Mount of Beatitudes Church on the Sea of Galilee's shores and that one of her boys, Yehezkel, would marry and raise a family in Israel?

Despite the long, long journey they shared, the brothers Yehezkel and Leon eventually parted, each marrying in a different country. Leon decided to return to France in 1947 where he met his wife, Ann, and married in 1957. At the age of 50, by some amazing miracle, Leon became a father when their only child, Marc, was born. He was my only Klebanov cousin.

During Israel's *Tzena*, a decade-long period of austerity which began in 1949 right after the 1948 War of Independence and following Leon's return to France, Abba would place a collect call to his brother. "May I speak with Benjamin?" he'd ask.

"No. There's no Benjamin here," Leon would respond.

Then the two, one in Tel Aviv, one in Paris, would put the phone receiver down, having ensured one another that they were fine while circumventing the hefty long-distance charges.

Abba would breathe a sigh of relief, his anxiety about his brother's welfare temporarily assuaged.

But God didn't entirely disappoint Abba, who had always held onto a sliver of faith. Had Frieda had an inkling of what was to become of her boys, she'd have taken a deep breath, filling her lungs with a surplus of oxygen and let out a long, relieving sigh, taking the weight off of her mind for at least a moment before her death.

Abba chose to live in Israel. A new beginning.

The letter he sent to the 'Yizhar' soaps and oils manufacturing plant requesting employment depicts his humility. The young and highly talented engineer writes that he is willing to work 'even in a simple job.'

***

Yehezkel Klebanov
4 Sirkin Street (c/- Berl)
Tel Aviv

Attn: The Management, Yitzhar Manufacturing Plant, Nahalat Yitzhak

I respectfully request a position in the manufacturing plant in one of your production branches doing any type of work. My health enables me to perform physical labor, and I am willing to take on even a simple job.

I state in advance that I am willing to accept the conditions of a new, base-level laborer in any position you may require.

As I have only recently arrived in Israel, I wish to take the liberty of referring, by name, to several acquaintances from Lithuania and France who can attest that I am a reputable and trustworthy individual.

Attached to this request are several certificates from my previous role in Spain.

Sincerely,
Yehezkel Klebanov

***

Frieda always knew that Yehezkel, from a very young age, was a resourceful little lad with a scientist's soul. When helping Freida in the kitchen, he was captivated by how ingredients blended into a new delicacy, checked the oven's temperature, ensured that the Shabbat challah braids were best positioned for optimal baking. Every new creation, both in nature and in the kitchen, excited him.

From my gray memory cells I fish out pictures and colors. I also stroke the tzigaleh and run the film in my mind in reverse: the Bobbeh I never had is looking at the paintings, smiling, and asks the eynikl she never had:

"You bring goats into the studio!?"

"I open the gate to the yard and you, Bobbeh, enter with all the family. The tzigaleh needs to be taken to the meadow. She's almost starving."

I tell my Bobbeh Frieda, as if she were a doting grandmother I had known and loved, about the movie 'Life is Beautiful.'

"Humor about the Shoah?"

"A bit of a smile won't hurt. I'm named after you, Aliza. Isn't that funny?"

The notebook once outlined with only black contours begins to flesh out. The colors on the page fill empty spaces and bring the faded, sketched memories to life. The words embroider a family.

A HOME IN A FILE FOLDER

In a cardboard file folder, its edges frayed, a thin elastic band attempting to hold its transparent pages together, lies a photograph of a single-story home looking more like a forlorn person trying to embody a page torn from history that no one has been able to comprehend.

In another photograph, four or five members of a family in bulky winter coats seem bewildered, as though about to travel to the land of oblivion. A one-way journey. A carriage harnessed to a weary horse takes them from their tiny home to the synagogue, where… the echoes of shots, a deafening silence hangs over the corpses of the innocent who have committed no crime.

The final chapter: A mass grave.

A SIXTH SENSE

There's no way of knowing for certain, but it's possible that I inherited my sixth sense from Bobbeh Frieda. Premonition, intuition, the ability to bypass the superfluous, a flash of claircognizance connecting with a specific person, non-linear thinking full of metaphors and vibrance. The comfort of knowing some matters will work themselves out on their own, and that sometimes making too much of an effort might sabotage the impending.

In my youth I fought this sixth sense but, in adulthood, as it developed and softened, it became a useful tool. When the mind cannot provide an answer, I place a hand on my abdomen and it answers in its own way: either with pain or joy. Keeping this sixth sense in good shape requires healthy logic and two feet planted firmly on the ground.

THE MAIN THING IS LOVE

Cock-a-doodle-doo. Gob-gob-gobble. I sincerely hope you haven't forgotten me! I must pop in now and say something. As I already told you, with time I became a Lithuanian hyndik. And now I've become, God save me, a scapegoat. Well, how can I put this: we're lucky that turkeys are heavy, and we can't easily be hoisted above any heads. But, in America, for their Thanksgiving holidays, we turkeys get slaughtered by the truck-load. That's the day that the Americans express gratitude to their God whereas we curse ours, even though it's the same God for everyone, and I know we shouldn't take his name in vain. It's lucky that Rabbi Haim can't hear me… but since the war… they've all disappeared, the whole world's changed. I don't want to talk about the war. And faith… yes, faith… well, we'll meet again and remember that the main thing is love.

This, too, I learned from Frieda.

LEON THE SMILING BROTHER, OR THE DALAI LAMA WHO DOESN'T DISAPPOINT

In the theatrical, poetic Russian film 'The Metamorphosis,' the jealous husband who suspects his wife of infidelity shoots several bullets towards a boat in which his wife and her male friend are sailing. The friend is hit in the heart; the boat, riddled with holes, begins filling with water; the heroine, unhurt, finds herself in the sinking vessel and lies across her lover, her eyes open. She sees no point in staying alive without him.

1940. Letters from Lena, the missing sister; a swastika embossed on the envelope. In small, crowded handwriting Lena tells about the final days of Vilna, about teaching. The brothers have difficulty reading between the lines.

By the written word, Lena is tightly holding on to life.

Lena and Yanek perished together in Lithuania.

***

After Abba passed away, Uncle Leon visited Israel every so often. I looked forward to those visits. I asked him to translate Lena's letters. Sitting together on the sofa, I opened a small packet which Abba had carefully kept.

"Could you read me a few of the letters?" I asked my uncle. I looked at him and asked once more. He said nothing.

"Could you perhaps read just one to me?"

I was so excited for the mysteries about to unravel, for the history, locked for decades in the drawer, to be brought to light. In just a moment, I'd know more. The secrets would slowly be revealed.

"Just one," he eventually said quietly.

After translating one letter I realized how difficult the experience was for him. Too difficult.

I could feel myself trying to please him. I wanted to know about the family but, at the same time, I could feel his pain over the loss. I tried to encourage and console. "Alright, that's enough for today. Tomorrow we can do another. One a day."

And my uncle answered, "You didn't mention homework. That's the last letter I'll read."

***

Leon didn't read any more of my aunt Lena's letters to me. He was insistent, like a schoolboy unwilling or unable to prepare assignments. I was sorry to have caused him pain. I'd hoped he would enjoy coming back to them, these letters that Abba saved. But Leon, as the younger one, wanted no responsibility. Solemnity and history were Abba's domain and, after his death, the package remained with me.

The Klebanov family's history burns hot, but is also fascinating, interesting, replete with wisdom, humor and the determination to survive.

A SCRATCHING SILENCE

There's no precise record. That leaves the pain hanging, suspended like a swinging pendulum with no conclusive answer. I can only presume the single and educated Lena, who was born in 1907 making her thirty four at the time, was murdered together with her parents and the townspeople. No death announcement, no epitaph, no account from Lena nor any neighbor, acquaintance or relative.

The silence scratches at the walls of comprehension.

No one ever went back to that home. No one has since seen the home, the kheider, or Bobbeh Frieda, who I never had and she never had me, nor Rabbi Haim, nor their pretty daughter, Lena.

But the tzigaleh had a life of her own, and she continues wandering around among the canvases, the paintings giving her and me a place and a space. I've never been there, but I go back without ever leaving my house. In my imagination and in the colorful paintings, people and flocks roam for eternity.

***

Bobbeh Frieda perished seven years before I was born. Somehow 'perished' sounds more appropriate than 'murdered,' even though it absolutely was outright murder, genocide. I never researched the Lithuanians. Instead of my feet and my soul traversing the archives and seeking the guilty, my heart leans less toward loathing and prefers to preserve my love, staying focused on the family.

REPARATIONS

How does one receive compensation for the deaths of your mother, father, and sister? For the loss of your house? How much is the home that anchors family worth? How much is life worth? A world destroyed?

We lived modestly. Most agreed to accept the reparations. But not Abba.

A TRANSPARENET CONNECTION

Two despondent people, Abba and I,

each with a camera and fountain pen in hand

beyond the hurdle of ashes cruelly separating

the fabrication of the past and the steep slope of the mountain

known as reality,

in the absence of miracles,

trying to document the transparent

PRIDE

I've only once heard Abba curse.

"*Reparations won't compensate for the loss of souls, not of a sister, not of a home, not of parents, and I will never accede to the Nazis,' may their names and memories be forever blotted out, presumption that a handful of banknotes will reimburse us for our losses, our treasures, the deaths of loved ones, for the blood that has been shed."*

He said his piece, then fell silent.

***

If not for his younger years being steeped in survival, Abba would likely have become a world- renowned researcher or top-class photographer. A notebook with a thick carton cover, embellished with his tidy handwriting and containing chemical formulae and delicate sketches of laboratory equipment is, to this day, among my favorite possessions. Just as he researched formulae and products, he researched his surroundings and the light.

His photos show his wonder at Orientalism, old Jaffa's alleys, the fishermen on the shoreline, sunrise, his perspective as sharp as his intellect. But something in his emotion faded. For many survivors, although their physical bodies survived, their souls, their emotions were taken from them. Like robots, they rose in the morning and went to work, successfully performing and completing tasks. They were reliable; as survivors, they were infinitely dedicated and focused on their job. Sleep, after a long day at work, was restless but served as a source of solace, a refuge from nightmares; dreams, if they did dream, sometimes revisited the nightmare.

In the morning, the sun rose anew, shining hope for a calm, routine day.

FURTHER

Abba and his brother never returned to Lithuania. They became ambivalent about the country they had loved deeply: although they never defamed it, they did claimed that the Lithuanians were worse than the Nazis. They didn't look back. The brothers strode swiftly ahead, always looking forward.

It took years to understand who Abba was. It always seemed to me that he held secrets.

Abba would say '*vayter*,' next, move forward, as though 'there' would be better. He always walked quickly and ahead of the family, clutching his camera like a secret weapon, looking for something new or fleeing from something old. I move forward and backward, as one and the same, back all the way to Bobbeh Frieda and forward in my life, with imagination and creations. Memory and imagination override the rules of logic: Frieda and I meet up, in fables and in paintings.

And this is how I became the last person able to tell the tale, even though I always wanted Leon to be the one telling it. Uncle Leon was the last Lithuanian. And that Lithuanian was as affectionate and lovable as he was obstinate and secretive. He preferred, perhaps rightly, to eat a fresh baguette, take a bite from a ripe wheel of Camembert or the old favorite '*rozhinkes und mandlen*,' raisins and almonds. He preferred to sip fine port wine than talk of the past. Abba didn't help much either. In a desperate attempt to erase the pain, as if pain can be erased, Abba spoke very little about the family in prewar times.

REWIND OR PARTISANS

A wish. If only I could find a letter which would reveal Bobbeh as a fighter and Zeideh as a Rabbi and partisan. The letter would say that Lena escaped to Israel under a false name. In another letter I'd read that Abba traveled to Lithuania and, with extraordinary timing, managed to help his parents escape. If that had been Abba's life he would have been able to show emotion towards his children. Perhaps my brother's tragic death might have been prevented.

A handful of Jews, some of whom were farmers, some landholders, some owners of flour mills, were hidden by non-Jewish neighbors, the goyim. But my Zeideh Rabbi Haim's family lived among Jews. No one could help them.

***

After the war, my parents lived their everyday lives.
Or so it seemed.

***

The rift cracked us from within.

***

The Shoah is still our European-Israeli rift. The war split many families' histories into two. In 1941, the continent was split into two banks, one on either side of the fault, so distant from each other that they formed an abyss.

The gap created between these two disconnected banks is so massive that we aren't able jump across it.

Writing attempts to scope out the dimensions of this abyss, to fill in the cracks.

Even though they never fought, I'm proud of my family. I'm proud of Abba, who did not live to his fullest capability and vitality, but was a wonderful father to his family. He did his absolute best, as do I.

TRAMPOLINE

The parents moved about like acrobats walking the one remaining wire of a tight-rope, afraid to fall into the abyss of memory.

The children were circus kids who were not amused by pets. Ours was a generation which wandered among the tents of faraway silences, pliable to the point of fearless of the supposed dangers. My mother wriggled like transparent modeling clay. Abba wasn't there; the house was hollow. The neighbor lady was scary. My brother disappeared.

So did I. And that's how I came to be with those that weren't, and those that were, who returned from there, made of some elastic material, so anguished and seemingly lacking a backbone.

You, Frieda, wonder of wonders: you would have understood what was about to occur, you would have sold the cow, the turkey and the goat and would have swiftly decided to escape with your husband and daughter; all three of you would have fled the town and travelled to America via France, collecting the two boys along the way. That way the family unit would have stayed together and you wouldn't have been counted among the annihilated. Everything would have turned out differently: I would've been happier, written less, as easygoing as the white goat on the grass in the sun, giving thanks to the Creator of the Universe.

APPLAUSE FROM THE AUDIENCE

In 'Fiddler on the Roof' all the residents of the *shtetl*, the little township of Anatevka in the Russian Empire, are ordered to leave. This is a very sad scene but, after they leave, they all scatter to various places around the world where they continue to live their lives. From the shtetl my family lived in, only ten people survived. Where are these ten? In the video I would prepare, the survivors reveal enigmas and tales about my family and about the shtetel. In the closing scene all the murdered townspeople come out from behind the wings, bowing and smiling to thunderous applause from the audience.

ZEIDEH DIDN'T GET FAR

When we were little, we'd recite all 22 letters of the Hebrew alphabet out loud as four words: '*Abg'dah, vazakh'ti, calmansa, patzkareshet.*' It helped us remember the correct sequence. Zeideh was halted mid-lesson, in the middle of the alphabet.

My Zeideh the Rabbi, who taught in kheider, *alef bet, kamatz patakh*, the alphabet, vowel chart, and how to pronounce them.

He didn't get far. The war cut him off in the middle; he never reached the last letter, *tav*.

***

The place where the massacre was carried out, 'B' for Babtai.

The town erased from the map, 'V' for 'Vandžiogala.'

It ends with an 'M' for 'massacre.'

The land where the massacre took place, an 'L' for Lithuania.

The number of slaughtered, an 'S' for six-hundred.

***

And I, daughter of Yehezkel, firstborn of Haim, too insignificant to bridge from B to Z, hear about how

Rabbi Haim Klebanov, my grandfather, fervently and wholeheartedly requests, beseeches, that I continue.

"Go on, continue, my eynikl. I've already used every letter, word, sentence and sketch to trigger your imagination; I cannot tell you anything, but there is a veiled way I can help you, and you'll only discover it if you write. Just write, my eynikl, do you hear me?"

"Truth be told, yes, Zeideh, I hear you."

My Zeideh doesn't leave me a choice. The letters he didn't have sufficient time to teach scream out, they beg. "We're looking for a place!"

And I capitulate, sitting and writing them, just so they will stop screaming.

A GRAVE DOESN'T HAVE TO BE OPENED FOR THE SPIRIT TO BE RELEASED

I don't need to find the actual place, dig in the dirt, wander among stones tinged by moss. Through a literary effort, sans searches and digging, I'm able to release Frieda's spirit from her grave.

Suddenly she pops up, her braids wrapped around her head like a crown, barefoot in her white dress, light as a feather, her smile heralds good tidings.

"Thank you." She breathes deeply.

"I waited for you. I wanted a Bobbeh."

"I've got an idea. Would you like to hover?"

"Hover? How?"

"You'll feel it, I'll help you. Smile at me. More. Shake off your shoes. Slip your socks off. Remove the silver chain. Raise your hands to the sides. More. A bit higher. Yes, that's good. Take a deep breath. Here, you see? Don't be scared. It's that simple!"

She pauses. "You have to believe," her boney fingertips brushing my skin. The body is so light, the head is relaxed, our hands spread to the sides. Now we glide. Flush to the clouds. Not even the birds can reach us. We sail through a cyan sky. What a tranquil silence. Every so often Frieda smiles at me.

"Hard to believe how pleasant it is, huh?"

HEAVEN

On the day my Zeideh Haim rose to heaven,
the Hebrew letters rose with him.
Up, up, not a mark was left, neither good nor bad.
Not a single letter.
On the day that Rabbi Haim rose to heaven,
the letters all rose to the cerulean heavens.
The heavens wept on the day that my Zeideh, Haim,
rose to meet them.

Gliding in quietude. Countless figures are gliding, dotting the viscous blue bed beneath the canopy of white stars. The letter shin, ש, stands out on the cubes of tefillin, the phylacteries, resting on Haim's forehead. The seven black leather bands wound around his forearm look like a ladder unraveling. The tzitzit, the long wool strings on the four corners of his tallit, his prayer shawl, move back and forth like angels' beating wings. His shoelaces flop to the sides. Threads and more threads unravel from Zeideh's image, and he himself slowly disentangles.

Frieda's headscarf gently touches his tzitzit. Her colorful dress billows with fresh air like a parachute. Lena's thick braids flutter in the wind, moving up and down like a bird's wings, shrouded in a veil so transparent that its white tinge can barely be seen, the sparkle of golden stars discernible through it.

The town's 600 perished residents follow after Haim, their Rabbi. He leads them all in a V formation, the letter ש guiding him through the convoluted heavens. As quiet as a flock of paper swans, they all fly eastward. Polite birds do not ask extraneous questions.

CHAGALL'S PAINTING

My right foot has no cushioning. I step on bones, on nerves, the pain piercing. I was meant to fly, to serve as a colorful image in a Chagall painting, to hover and glide through purple skies alongside the white goat, adjacent to the fiddler in his white frock coat. In the background Mozart's Requiem plays. My bird's eye view shows me the gray Lithuanian town. I don't swoop: God forbid I could step on bones; I don't enter the garden, I don't open the door, I don't stand on my foot because I don't want to slip, so close to the bones that it hurts. Yes, being close hurts.

From my bird's-eye view I am privy to the following scenario: in his chambers, Schäfer converses with the Führer, initially hinting to him, and then says quite emphatically that Hitler has gone too far; the Führer strokes his mustache, makes an effort to think logically, and quite surprisingly orders the Lithuanians to leave the Jews alone.

This snippet of information reaches Himmler, who advises the Führer that such a decision regarding Lithuania's Jewish population overall, and the smattering of Jews in Vandžiogala in particular, is one of the smartest decisions he has made, because eradicating the last 600 Jews, who are unarmed and trapped in the tiny synagogue of the tiny town of Babtai, is not just cruelty for cruelty's sake, but rather brutality. Hitler thanks Himmler for supporting his plan to temporarily cancel the pinpointed eradication. The Jews of Vandžiogala are saved.

All at once, life's blush returns to the gray township.

***

Unlike Fellini's film 'Amacord' where the penetrating light causes the colors to dissipate, in the town's case the penetration of light empowers the colors. Everything begins to bustle with life, tones and hues.

The Lithuanian soldier puts his weapon down, signals to Haim to open the synagogue's gates; Haim does as he's told, opens the gates and the townsfolk exit silently, all but one woman who sobs, "Unbelievable. Unbelievable. A miracle. Truly a miracle!"

Haim approaches the soldier and whispers. "Godspeed."

The townsfolk scatter to their homes to discover that no one had invaded their houses in their absence. The synagogue was not turned into a cowshed. Tombstones do not adorn the pathways of the homes of non-Jews. The streets buzz with activity, filled with people, with horses and donkeys. The wagoner feels triumphant and says to the farmer, "I told you, it was all just hearsay."

The fair returns to town. The market is jam-packed. Once again, the cacophony of pots gurgling on stoves, griddles and wooden spoons bring the aromas of cooking to the fore. Frieda, in her floral apron, dashes off to the cow, to the hyndik and, lastly, to the tzigaleh. Hugging the tzigaleh she whispers into its neck:

"Hello, my lovely one. What, did you think I'd leave you? That humans could be so cruel? Really, we had two very tough weeks, but you see… you have to believe!"

The wagoner whistles to his horse. "Giddy-up, giddy-up, you lazy thing, you. Get going!"

Haim smooths his coat, shaking off his thoughts. Children have noticed that the Rabbi has come home, doors open and children spill out of their houses at a run, huffing and puffing, clutching at Haim's coat, hugging him.

"Come, my little clowns, let's go to the kheider. We'll pick up where we left off."

Haim continues teaching the Hebrew letters, from *bet* to *tav*. Summer goes by pleasantly. At Rosh Hashanah, the Jewish New Year, Haim again teaches the story of the world's creation. Eve doesn't tempt Adam with an apple, the snake catches a mouse and slithers off in a different direction while Adam and Eve take a stroll through the Garden of Eden. Haim hugs his children and his pupils and kisses the tops of their heads.

"The earth continues to spin on its axis," he says, "and time flashes by so quickly. Look, it's already the month of *Tishrei* once again."

"Tateh," Yehezkel retorts, "time doesn't go any faster than it always has, it's just your perception of time."

"My smart little boy. You're right, of course. Something went a bit askew in my timekeeping. It's hard to explain."

Haim, deep in thought, strokes his beard.

***

Rosh Hashanah has come to Vandžiogala. The townspeople prepare for the festivities, feverishly cleaning their homes; the women excitedly sew new clothes. For the evening meal they cook special holiday dishes: sweet scents of braided challah breads and honey and ginger *sausainiai* waft from Frieda's kitchen. Lena, sitting on the tree stump outside, chats to Yanek who has recently recovered from tuberculosis. They go inside and announce their engagement. A tear drops onto Frieda's cheek.

"Well, well. So we need to write a *vort*, the betrothal agreement. And call the klezmers to come and play some merry *freilach* songs."

Haim sighs and asks, "What's the rush? There's plenty of time," scratching his head as he goes back to reading the book of *Bereshit*, Genesis. "In the beginning God created… and the earth was without form and void."

"Oy. Rabbi. The flood will come soon," a child whispers fearfully.

Haim ponders and answers slowly, as though wanting to add a question mark to the end of his words but leaving, instead, a period. "Patience, little one. There's an order to the world."

***

That's what my Zeideh thought. Zeideh, on whom war, not peace, fell; who was pure, and required to serve as an exemplar of order. Zeideh obeyed instructions and led the community to the synagogue in Babtai, remaining forever with his faithful congregation.

SPRATS, BEETS AND MOZART'S REQUIEM

Because of my much-loved uncle Leon, Abba and I became Francophiles, in love with the culture and the language - the true love language with which the brothers conversed with each other. Over time I joined their conversations in French. The sound of French is delightful, inspirational; as one for whom it is not mother tongue, I frequently hear things differently. For instance, the French word for beetroot is *betterave*. I have no idea of the word's etymology, but to me it sounds like '*beit HaRav*' which, in Hebrew, means 'the Rabbi's home' and brings to mind the home of my Zeideh, of blessed memory.

Slowly the entire musical requiem was intertwined with loss, with the taste of pickled beets, imported from France and labeled, in my associative thoughts, as 'the Rabbi's home.' As for the sprats from Riga, nostalgia draws me to the shelf in the store and the taste, despite the distance, raises thoughts that Zeideh and I have enjoyed the same foods. Cyrillic letters stir a longing for a different life, for the connections, the sights, the tastes which I never had the privilege of experiencing. Without a headstone, the final resting place becomes transient. Every stone brings something forgotten to mind.

The heritage was cut short.

BOBBEH'S SOUP RECIPE

Aya, who immigrated to Israel from Japan, has a secret recipe for miso soup with tofu, her great-grandmother's recipe. She's proud of the soup she makes in the restaurant, and the tale adds a special flavor that warms the heart.

Herbert cherished the feather quilt that his grandmother gave him. It was the only keepsake he had of her. When he immigrated to Israel there was no room for it in the freight container and he had to leave it behind. For years Herbert gets cold at night whenever he thinks of the quilt that remained in Argentina.

Stories about grandmothers bring smiles; the scent of her face powder, the feel of her consoling caress, flavors of what's cooking and baking in her warm kitchen. My Bobbeh bequeathed me nothing other than excerpts of stories about her, told to me by Abba in a sentence, or maybe two.

Sadness is elusive. I resuscitated my Bobbeh Frieda, I created additional tales so that she'd continue to sit next to me, holding my hand.

"*Gezundheit!*" Bobbeh Frieda would say when I sneezed. "A sign that everything's true."

"Not everything," I answered. "Some of the stories are '*bubbe meises*,' old wives' tales."

"If I, your Bobbeh, say they're true, believe me."

I smiled and believed. After all, I was the one who

dressed my real Bobbeh in an imaginary frock and apron, reinventing her. Meanwhile, I construct a model of a wise, affectionate Bobbeh: she has an answer to every question that comes up; she's an experienced chef who's just taken comforting ginger snaps from the oven. My Bobbeh smells like face powder, vanilla and cinnamon.

LONELINESS

Abba takes solace in a slice of bread. It's what he needed, other than everything else he needed which he'll never again have. He always said *'a shtikeleh broit.'* Again and again the tips of his long fingers would mush the slice of bread before he lifted it to his mouth. His fingertips left crumbs on the table; they shaped miniature statuettes from the bread. It seemed to be a movement that was almost inherent to his fingers.

His brother would also mush the bread and he, too, was satisfied with just one slice. Bread was the foundation, sometimes accompanied by red wine, Camembert or Roquefort. He didn't care if the slice was dry or if it was predominantly the crust; even a faint greenish tinge didn't bother him. He'd just say, "it's penicillin, excellent immunization; after all, penicillin is intentionally inserted into Roquefort to enhance its flavor."

And indeed, we never got sick. We were inoculated. We'd shower in cold water only twice a week, on Mondays and Thursdays. In all honesty, we were well-bolstered, primarily our bodies.

Like many educated Jews, Abba adopted a far-left sociopolitical ideology. Among the activists he was considered a 'living room communist': not too active. Berl, the neighbor in the house across the street from us, edited the newspaper

'Voice of the People,' initially published by the Palestine Communist Party and, later, the Israel Communist Party.

Abba and Berl found a common language and became friends. Years later he'd say, "when you're young, if you aren't a communist, you have no heart but, when you're older, if you're still a communist, you have no brain." Abba's sharp mind quickly found the twist in every situation.

As an engineer, Abba was a member of the Freemasons. A small wooden cupboard had just enough space for a secret cape. Abba was adept at connecting the materialistic with the philosophical, as he did laughter with sorrow, practicality with integrity, in his never-ending attempt to assimilate his family's brief history. Reality became fiction, fiction became truth, truth melted into insufferable pain. Bread always comforted him. Abba ached the pain of the past, the pain of the present, the dizzying speed at which reality faded away. To his last day he searched for what was lost, for meaning.

THE SEARCH BUREAU FOR MISSING RELATIVES

Abba left many questions unanswered and losses sans addresses. And I, like Zeideh, move restlessly around the ruined walls. Seeking in vain that which is lost, not unlike the Search Bureau for Missing Relatives.

As a war orphan, Abba tried to belong, to fit in, modulating his love of isolation with socializing. His entire life he endeavored to fix things. Abba fixed scuffed shoes. He'd put the shoe on a metal stand, attach a crescent of metal to the worn-down sole and, clutching the nails between his lips, hammered them one by one with stunning precision. When the shoe pressed on the big toe, he cut the shoe's tip with a sharp knife, removing a perfect crescent. Toes could peep out undisturbed, concealing secrets about families that survived even though, or perhaps because, they had no money to buy new shoes.

For years Abba went about asking: where are my glasses? Where is the camera? Where are the shoes? Where are the keys? There was no one he could turn to and ask: where is my sister, my mother, my father?

Like the glasses which he sought for years, perched on the crown of Abba's head,
So it was with death: of his family, which suddenly disappeared, never to be seen again.
It stained the air; and Abba, a wise man, could not fathom death because he couldn't see it or shake its hand goodbye. One who cannot comprehend that is unable to live.
We saw the glasses on his head as a mark of Cain; but Abba, his mind weighted with thoughts, kept searching.

A TRUE STORY ABOUT A DIFFERENT GRANDFATHER

The search is endless. Where are the eyeglasses, the shoe, the camera, the keys, the quiet, the restfulness and, above all,
"Loif ich heikher, ibber dekher, on in zukh vu bist tu vu?" Abraham Sutzkever, the famed Lithuanian poet, wonders in Yiddish, but the translation lacks the same flow:
"I run higher, over roofs, and I'm looking: where are you, where?"

***

Anyone listening to the song "Beneath the Splendor of Heaven's Stars" in Hebrew, and all the more so in Yiddish, cannot remain unmoved. It was penned in the Vilna Ghetto. Sutzkever, a partisan who experienced loss after loss there, continued living and laughing by virtue of his writing. His poems are an anchor for the soul.

Who will remain, what will remain?
Another syllable remains
To sprout its creation
Which from the start He creates.

In the daytime a funeral, and a concert at dusk.
To be here and be there, so heaven proclaimed.
It was decreed that from the shoulders they'll be hung
Replete with sorrow and joy: two pails.

On the evening marking the thirty days since his passing, Israeli actress and writer Hadas Kalderon spoke about her grandfather, Avraham (Avrasha) Suskever:

"My grandfather told me three stories. I'm very proud of him. He described how he left the town and began crossing a bridge when suddenly he saw a uniformed Nazi standing before him. He had no way out. Avrasha focused his blue-eyed gaze on the Nazi's blue eyes and innocently asked, 'Do you know which way I need to go so there won't be any Nazis?' Stunned, the soldier pointed in a certain direction. 'I hit him with a psychological shocker,' my grandfather said.

"After crossing the bridge, Avrasha didn't know where to go. As a poet, he decided to walk as far as the seventh street and enter the thirteenth house. And so he did.

"He knocked on the door and met a woman who hid him for several months in the basement, and that's how he was saved.

Another story he told described how he and his wife Frieda were taken by plane from the forest so that he could save his poems and bring them to the Russian side."

That's not my Zeideh's story. His wife was named Frieda, but Avrasha's Frieda made it to Israel.

A HOME FOR THE PAIN

I try to set the pain down on the page; it self-replicates, again, again, and again.
I build it a poem-house and it cuts itself a path back to my heart.
I crack a window open for it and the pain bursts forth from the corridor.

TAKEOFFS AND LANDINGS

In the expanse of imagination, security checks are extraneous. I march energetically through Vilna's streets. In the background the Red Army Choir sings. Heavy boots encase my feet; a thick coat wraps my body. Suddenly, my friend Vanya is right in front of me. He's clutching a multi-hued bag which, I'm happy to discover, holds well-wrapped, beautiful handmade babushkas I'd once asked him for. Nice that he remembered. I thank him, and he asks:

"Why so formal?"

"Not formal," I answer. "Just moved."

Suddenly the two of us break into raucous laughter. We quickly head to the city's plaza. Vanya suggests we go for a vodka at the Petroika Bar. On the way he meets a friend and shouts, "Tovarish!" and the friend waves to us. Vanya joins the friend and calls out to me:

"Masha, don't worry, my girl. I'll come later. I've set up a chess game with Pieter."

As his shadow distances in the darkness, I pull my hat down over my ears, laughing aloud. My breath makes an unexpected ice flower in the air. Streams of nostalgia and the poetic songs of George Brassens emerge: I'm in Paris, adorned in a red dress with a deep encolure, high-heeled shoes, clutching a warm baguette which I've bought fresh at the boulangerie. Striding towards me is Janeau: so affable, a dimple appears in his right cheek when he smiles. He's wearing a blazer, a beret and, with a huge smile, presents me with a bouquet of purple lavender spreading a heady scent. I close my eyes. Janeau is free and joins me and, off we go, arm in arm down the avenue. He quotes Jacques Prévert, "A million years are not enough to describe the moment of eternity when I kissed you…" and suddenly he does, he kisses me.

I become weak in the knees, and he supports me. We're so light and blissful.

"What's the occasion?" I ask.

"Vera, I don't know… the flowers are for your birthday."

"I forgot… but now that I think about it, today is not my birthday."

"So why did I think it was today?"

"The truth is, something did happened today… something else."

"Want to tell me? I'm a philosopher, not a detective. Or have you forgotten?"

"Thanks for the good wishes. The truth is, your timing is perfect."

"So I noticed. I missed you… when you were away… where did you go?"

"I thought… I wrote… I was totally immersed in a different country, Lithuania."

I burst out of the chasm and into the present.

"Vera, you're so predictable, Lithuania of all places… of all the places in the world? Either way, I'm happy you're back."

Janeau whispers in my ear, and I smile. He blows me a kiss and runs off to a meeting.

"*Au revoir*," he shouts.

"See you!" I answer, thinking that nothing is certain.

The Spanish music is seductive and suddenly I'm a flamenco dancer, voluminous red skirts wrap around my thighs, Flamenco heels clacking quickly and powerfully on the wooden floor. My blue-black hair is pulled back tight, adorned with a red ribbon, a lace fan in hand. Antonio flashes me a sly look and the music from the Concierto de Aranjuez drives us mad. Guitar players step towards us, urging us to dance. Antonio invites me with an outstretched hand.

"Sylvia! C'mon! You're so beautiful today. It's a day for dancing!"

He holds me firmly. His hand almost encircles my narrow waist. We're carried away into the wild dance, to the onlookers' cheers. I'm flooded with joy, I wave my wide skirt around, clicking my castanets. "Ole!" Antonio shouts. The crowd wants an encore but we quickly disappear behind the curtain.

***

Hustle and bustle. The noise of car engines, children shouting. Newspapers with gaping black eyes. Tension. Sweltering heat. A strange smell.

I burnt the food.

Where have I been? Maybe I was submerged in the jumble of languages. Yes, I was buried in a landslide of words. Every day I pass through at least four countries, every day I prepare for and make the journey, taking the routes that Abba took, and neither of us reach our desired destination. I don't need jets and airports. In the air I feel tranquil, but landings are tough. Every once in a while I'm hit hard in the belly. The empty space left by Frieda is far larger than I'd thought.

Frieda, the ubiquitous grandmother, has one granddaughter whose presence multiplies like a kaleidoscope, from Masha into Vera and Sylvia to Aliza. Each of the women, the Lithuanian, the French, the Spanish, the Israeli, is searching for Frieda so that she can collapse into her warm bosom. Each of the granddaughters is searching for herself, for her identity. The search, which has become frantic, becomes a being in and of itself.

CHILDREN OF IMMIGRANTS, TRANSITIONING FROM THERE TO HERE

Betach, betach, tznon va'retekh. The literal translation is 'sure, sure, radish and radish'; well, it sounds funnier in Hebrew as it rhymes, but anyway, it's a phrase used as a mocking response, 'you're talking nonsense.' When they came to Israel, Abba, his brother and their acquaintances spoke in a concoction, mingling Yiddish with Hebrew. 'Sure, sure, *tznon va'retekh*' is a silly phrase, a tautology, as 'radish' in Hebrew is '*tznon*' and, in Yiddish, '*retekh*.'

When modern Israel was established, laborers called any tool for which they didn't know the correct Hebrew name a '*makhoutel*': "Can you hand me the makhoutel please?" It was some kind of hybrid between a *mastrina*, in Arabic, and *shpachtel*, in Yiddish, a kind of graft between a plier and a pincer. Many tools were still known by their German names. Laborers spoke in their temporary languages until the Hebrew eventually became fluent. It was a transition period, between the 'old country' and the land where they began a new life. Between Jewish and Arab laborers. As the kids of immigrants from European and other countries, we also blended words from other languages.

My mother sent me to the corner grocery store with a list: bread, milk and zemelbreizel. When it was my turn, that's what I asked the shopkeeper for, 'bread, milk and 'zemelbreizel' A plump woman laughed and, in a teacher's tone of voice, she said, "Ah, cutie. You must have wanted to say breadcrumbs, am I right, little one?" And I said, "Yes, thank you." The weeping little girl went running home, all the way down Hashmonaim Street, clutching a basket with very few items in it.
A girl too short by seven centimeters.

***

Yiddish, with its soft sounds, merges joy and sorrow, juicy jokes, the sounds of a loving Bobbeh. One of my favorite things to do of late is to receive text messages in Yiddish from my close girlfriend. On a cellphone these Yiddishisms are doubly amusing, and brightens my day.

"*Kleiner dem oilem, greisser di simcha.*" The smaller the world, the greater the joy.

"*Ikh veykh nisht alt, ikh vahks tsureik; vee a koyzeh, ober khap akouk oif yenem.*" I'm not getting old, I'm aging in reverse like a calf, but get a look at that one!

Hebrew is an ancient, rich language but when I can't find a word, I draw from Yiddish and French. Hebrew, integrated with other languages, alludes to a secret doorway, like in Alice in Wonderland.

The power of imagination allows me to soar off into the heavens, to sail on the white pages, to crawl into the secret cave, to sift through sand for colorful seashells. I take Frieda along for the ride, lifting her off the ground, above the harsh, demanding reality.

EUROPE IN TEL AVIV

A country in its infancy.
In the 1950s in little Tel Aviv, the milkman rang the bell on Sunday and left milk bottles next to the doors; the kerosene man rang the bell on Monday; the ice man rang the doorbell on Tuesday. Each day the neighbors came out: Dezhlovski, Minkowsky, Poczimak, Labnowski, Kolbowski, Dorembous, Weidel. This one went to the local grocer, that one to the fish monger, this one brought ice, another returned from work by bus, Eli Weidel licked the walls, the neighbor said he was low on calcium, the twins Gabbi and Shalom argued. One mother called; "Harmona, come for afternoon snack!" Marika got pregnant, her family left the neighborhood. The neighbors felt as though they were a small community.

Abba trimmed the trees in the small yard facing the apartment while he dreamed of Frieda's garden in Lithuania. In the apartment facing east lived Manya and Yosh Halevi. She was a Shoah survivor from Poland, the actress and playwright who wrote "Dalia and the Sailors" and he was the editor of Ma'arachot magazine. Opposite them lived Berl, editor of the communist newspaper. On the first floor lived Levi Eshkol's wife. Kids went to school in clothes sent to them from America.

When the school bell rang, children would obediently

file into the classrooms. At recess, a teacher would check children's heads with glass combs, looking for lice and, on another break, pupils collected horse manure for the school garden. Excited parents from Poland, Romania, Hungary and Lithuania waited in their homes, not knowing what a healthy sandwich is; they learned new Hebrew words from their children; mothers wore aprons and took a siesta between two and four in the afternoon.

All the modest apartments looked alike, with overcrowded shelves of books in a variety of languages. Sonia the Crazy ran up and down Rothschild Boulevard, and Yankel Dudu was seen coming and going, making strange gestures next to the park in Lunz Street. Sonia died by suicide. It was because of that war. Solly, the librarian, an old bachelor, lived with his even older mother and wouldn't allow swapping more than one book a day. The butcher woman fell in love with the barber, the barber won the lottery together with the artist Yossl Bergner. The children in the corner house came down with polio.

Little by little the neighborhood transformed; the local grocer closed down and, instead, a sex store opened. Neighbors protested. The place where people brought their wet laundry to hang dry became a café. Labnowski became Livneh, Gerstenfeld became Paltiel, Einshtein became Elad. Yanek became Yossi, Yuri became Uri, Klebanov stayed Klebanov.

I was named after Frieda.

HOW MANY JEWS PERISHED IN THE HOLOCAUST

A few years back on Holocaust Remembrance Day I arrived at the kindergarten where I work as an art therapist. After the siren was sounded, the kindergarten teacher spoke about the Shoah.

A lovely child with sparkling eyes came over to me excitedly, endeavoring to convey what he felt about the experience of the morning. In his sweet child's voice, he asked me:

"Do you know how many Jews were killed in the Shoah?" he asked.

"How many?" I played dumb.

"Six Jews!" he said, in a serious tone infused with sorrow. "Six. That's a lot, right?"

"Yes," I smiled at him.

This was during one of the Intifada periods when there were terror attacks almost daily, and six people killed was indeed horrific. You can't weigh six million on a scale, the number is too large to comprehend. Six hundred thousand, sixty thousand, six thousand, six hundred, sixty.

Six people is indeed a lot, and not just for a very small child.

Three people in my own family, murdered in the Shoah, is an immeasurable abyss for me.

CONSTANT VS. VARIABLE

Constancy conveys stability. When a mother says, "I'll be back in a moment," the child believes her.

Constants are like an old, faithful friend, like the northern star, a large wagon, an entire neighborhood, a golden peacock, a home, an armchair, candlesticks, a Menorah, a song, the book 'The Day Never Ends,' herring, an embroidered tablecloth, apple strudel, a chunk of bread, *rozhinkes und mandlen*, compote made of dried fruit, a Leica or Zorki camera, hopscotch, playing jacks, a silver brooch, a Jaeger-LeCoultre watch, a Parker 51 fountain pen.

Contrary to her normal behavior, a mother made a promise, but did not fulfill her promise. No one returned. Permanent became temporary. The relocation was unintended. A family is buried together in a mass grave. The home is no more. All that it held is no more. The sacred artifacts are no more. Even longing no longer knows where to turn.

HOW TO SWEETEN?

How to sweeten? Lithuanians sweeten things with something small, concentrated. At the end of the meal a glass of colorless tea; no flour means no sausainiai dripping with cream; sweetening with a pinch of jam on a teaspoon, altering the tea's flavor. *Imberlakh,* a tangy sweet made of carrot, orange rind, ginger brittle and nuts, a piquant sweetener, sharp, intense, burning the tongue.

My other grandfather, my mother's father, was a baker and enjoyed a long life. From him I inherited my love of baking. In mornings when I was free, I wrote down wise sayings and on Fridays I baked cakes and sausainiai. Both my grandfathers, one in the spirit world and one in the material, encouraged me as they hovered, a pair of angels, each on either side of me.

Frieda, in her apron, pops into my kitchen to give me tips on how to get my sausainiai nice and crisp.

THE SECRET OF BIBLICAL JOY

My daughter wasn't a fan of the best-seller, 'The Secret,' claiming that the book wasn't for her. For an entire year I researched the biblical Secret and discovered that the content of 'The Secret' is drawn from Jewish sources. At some point later in time, I penned 'The Secret of Biblical Joy.' During the intense writing, I could feel Zeideh, Rabbi Haim Klebanov, sitting alongside me, sending me his knowledge, dictating Torah explanations and the wisdom of our sages. Even though he was the grandfather I didn't have, I felt his warm, spiritual closeness.

That's how I acquired a Zeideh.

DREAM

In my dream I suddenly turn old in a single day. My daughter says I've aged, my son also says I've aged and, in the mirror, my hair is unkempt and my face is wrinkled. I wake and am happy to see that I don't look the way I did in the dream. I wonder about Bobbeh Frieda, who never had the chance to get old, and my face gets mixed up with hers. It's as though she's writing the text.

I've been living through Frieda for a while now, writing and thinking about her. She, absent from my life for sixty years, pops up in all her glory and vibrance and, despite this new proximity, I need to form a divide between her and me.

FROM PAINTING TO WRITING TO PAINTING

The subjects of many of my paintings were a goat, a turkey, an old-fashioned house, and they'd jump up in front of me when I began unraveling the webs of my thoughts as I geared up to write tales about the goat and Bobbeh Frieda, who I never had. One of the paintings expresses longing: it's my Zeideh's coat, left hung on a hanger, his desk loaded with books, a simple pink room, and the goat worriedly peeking in from the outside. Thought and imagination shift between visual and verbal, between the little that's left and everything that is no more.

THE GOLD DOESN'T FEAR THE MELTING POT

And if the truth should come to light, any truth, a photo of Frieda's house, biographical details?

Would such a truth invalidate the biography I dreamt up? Or perhaps the truth and the fiction could live side by side like sisters, but which would be authentic? Would it be 'the' truth? Is there such a truth? After all, each of us sees things differently: Frieda, the turkey, the goat, the cow… would the truth refute or confirm the fiction, if it is, indeed, fiction? Would anyone discover the difference between the two? If falsity is the opposite of truth, and there is no source of information, it would be impossible to discern between what is true and what is false. One of these days it all might be overturned, and truth will become fiction, the fiction will become truth. Just like the dripping wax of a burning candle, after the candle has melted, we can collect the remnants, insert a new wick and create a new candle, one that is stronger and more beautiful than the one before.

Each of us has our own truth and even in the Register of Lithuanian Jewry, a serious, historic document, there are distortions: those closest to the writers and editors made sure to have their family's history logged; and for those who weren't, there's no mention or memory of the family. History, written by researchers and historians, sometimes brings injustice to truths and joy to lies, depending on how it is read and by whom.

Truth and fiction are a homogenous mixture of two alloys. The truth is horrifying, inconceivable, and consolidates with the plot of an imaginary childhood. In the Registrar of Communities, the memories and thoughts are blended together. For those family members who are no more, they were never awarded a prize, a medal, no one wrote of them in a newspaper, no one named a street for them, they were killed even though they were never in the battle. They never even got their own private burial plot. But here, in this story, they get top billing, starring roles, they are documented and recorded within this tapestry of words I embroidered to keep them safe.

EMOTIONAL INHERITANCE

Parents pass much more than just their DNA to their offspring. Habits become traditions. For years I found myself walking paths and fields with friends and neighbors where I am always on their left. I find it hard to walk with someone who's on my left. I need to be on the left. This flicker of memory connects, once again, to Lithuania.

As a robust, athletic young man, Abba jumped into freezing whitewater rapids and lost hearing in his right ear. He never said a word about it; in his stoic silence and with the slightest touch, he would very gently orient me to stand on his left so I could talk to his left ear; this was way before he ever told me about me the impediment, so I was used to him being on my right when we spoke. Since childhood, this practice became the norm: I would instinctively position myself to the left of my friends. Perhaps this was an unconscious choice on Abba's part, having realized that although he wouldn't hear bad news through his left ear, he wouldn't ever hear the good news either.

Sometimes a habit inadvertently becomes a tradition. As a daughter and her mother are preparing soup, strictly following the grandmother's recipe, they automatically chop off the chicken wings and toss them away. One day, the daughter asks her mother, "Why must we throw out the wings?" The mother, having done this for years, has no answer. So she asks the grandmother why the wings had to be discarded, and the grandmother answers, "The wings?... it's not necessary... ah, yes... the only pot I owned was too small, and the chicken wouldn't go in whole, so... I had to make it fit." A tradition set in stone; its origins - misinterpretation.

I SEWED A BOBBEH

When the custom of passing on traditions is thwarted before its time: recipes, jokes, etc. and heirlooms are not handed down: art, jewelry, candlesticks, Judaica, embroideries… when these have all disappeared, grandchildren are left with nothing other than to invent a past, to conjure up out of thin air traditions that would serve as a foundation for the next generation.

I stitch a custom-made dress of reality for Frieda. The mannequin I use is made from snippets of information. With nothing to work with aside from these scraps, I have no Bobbeh; this labor of love, sewing and writing, makes Frieda accessible and turns me into her eynikl. Some grandmothers sew a doll for their little girl; I sewed a grandmother. Now I have a Bobbeh. Bobbeh Frieda.

BIRTHDAY BALLOONS

On birthdays we ceremoniously inflate colorful balloons, blowing them up with all the air in our lungs to bring joy to the one whose special day it is, decorating the room in their honor. At the end of Frieda's life, no one attended her funeral because no there was no funeral. I never celebrated Frieda's birthday, and not just because she was murdered before I was born.

I only heard a smattering of phrases about her. Now I'm metaphorically puffing oxygen into the words and giving Frieda a gift: a virtual existence made of patches and remnants of the Bobbeh I was never privileged to have. I celebrate, very belatedly, this birthday for my new Bobbeh. By virtue of the air, time and love I devote to her, Frieda starts to come into being, spiritually. I restore all those years that I never felt, never said 'Bobbeh Frieda.' Now I'm writing it: Bobbeh Frieda.

MAKING DO WITH WHAT YOU HAVE

On Sukkot, the Feast of Tabernacles, the golden etrog, the citron, nests in its magnificent box of pure silver, an artisan's handiwork specially designed to fit the fruit in all its splendor. Tenderly, taking care that the pistil remains intact, the fruit is set down on a soft bed; the vessel is closed gently so that it won't, heaven forbid, be damaged. But no one designed a precisely shaped receptacle into which we can gently set our pain.

Following a spate of preparations, the celebratory concert was underway when suddenly a string on Yitzhak Perlman's violin snapped. The audience gasped as one. Perlman signaled to the conductor and continued playing his violin, less one string.

When the concert ended, he addressed the audience. "You know, sometimes it's the artist's task to find the music he can still produce with what is at hand." Thunderous applause ensued from the audience, concerned at the moment that the string had snapped that he may need to reattach his leg braces and go off to look for another violin.

World-class chefs know how to concoct delicacies from leftovers. The French have a recipe for stale bread. I create a story from scraps, using the leftovers to shape a cogent plot. I produce the custom-made vessel precisely shaped to house the longing.

FAREWELL

It's hard to talk about farewells without saying anything about Frieda. If no one is aware of the death, did it actually happen? Can you prove a negative? Like the mark left when a flower vase is removed from a dusty mantel, signaling its former presence, rather than no sign whatsoever to indicate it was ever there at all.

To start the process of saying farewell, there must be a need to disconnect, a feeling that someone is about to travel somewhere, to leave, a feeling that a person is ill, fighting for their life, close to death. Sometimes farewells take place naturally, without drama; the farewell of lovers; a slow, natural procedure, like fruit falling from the tree at the peak of ripeness.

Farewells occur when the gaps between meetings grow longer, until they are no more, like chewing gum stretched until it's so thin that it tears. There was no farewell from Frieda nor from her family. History barreled on with no chance to go back, to regret, to forgive; no final glance, touch, or embrace. There was no farewell nor any condolence message acknowledging that a close loved one was honored with a beautiful eulogy or respectable burial.

Yehezkel and Leon never got to say goodbye and part from their mother, not in any appropriate or respectful way. Frieda and her family never got to say a proper, final goodbye to other family members, to their surroundings, to neighbors.

The separation was forced on the family and the sons.

LIGHT AND FRIENDSHIP

The rite of passage for Ethiopian boys sees closest friends separated for eternity, the objective being to prevent them down-spiraling into argument and, instead, preserve the ideal friendship forever.

Love that ends without hurt or insult endures, like in the movie 'Casablanca.' Farewells, often unavoidable, leave those who loved still loving, even when the distance between them keeps growing. A ball of light continues rolling on, lighting the darkness even when those who love close their eyes.

Frieda, who spent so many years in the dark, was lit up by this ball of light. My relationship with her became a two-way street, so to speak, emotions echoing like a ball thrown forcefully against the wall. The wall's role, to return the ball, is huge. I am thankful every time flashes of light are reflected back to me.

AN ACT OF LOVE

Writing can be an exciting encounter with a loved one, a mindful process through which people can see themselves in their entirety. The loved one reflects the true self, the authentic, original self. Silence isn't frightening, as the encounter itself fills the empty space. The irises of our eyes meet and rekindle an extinguished flame. Writing gathers the puzzle pieces of my biography that had been lost for years.

And so, with classical music playing in the background, in my wonderful palace, I climb the imaginary flight of stairs to meet my Bobbeh. I descend into the darkest basements to check whether the roots are disrupting the palace's foundation or supporting its walls. In the parlor of my palace, I screen a private film which no one else can watch. In the dining room I improvise a meal from leftovers in the Lithuanian kitchen. Pursued by spirits, I climb again into the palace turret to gaze at the horizon and breathe in ash-free air.

In this gorgeous palace, when I move, it's like dancing around with my family. The silence in this palace clears my mind, makes my thoughts productive, my open eyes comprehending what my closed eyes saw. The sadness makes way for color, for laughter. Bereavement steps aside, kicked by the deadly demon of life. I breathe life into the corpses; I dress them in simple clothes, aprons, or special Shabbat clothes and, suddenly, they rise and go off to the market or to synagogue, laughing and running about in the yard, go inside the house and back out to the garden, bumping into the goat, the cow, and the turkey so tall it can eat right from the table.

Terms like 'persecutors,' 'Nazis' and 'cruelty' don't scratch the surface; even the word 'Holocaust' has become as perfunctory as an old, barbed wire fence.

The murderous Lithuanians can't believe their eyes. After all, they themselves methodically and efficiently eradicated all the town's residents, committing acts of cruelty and murder, all the while enjoying the process - taunting and laughing as they slaughtered people. They are perplexed. How the hell did these Jews come rise from the dead and come back to life?

Bereavement cannot cope with imagination. The purveyor of reality and fiction will sometimes confuse the two, turn back a page, and remember the fiction and forget the reality, or vice versa, asking at the end of the narrative: Really?! Only acts of love inspire the imagination, the soul, the spirit.

From the rusty barbed wire fence a green branch sprouted.

BELONGING

The terms 'belonging' and 'presence' complete each other. It's better to be present, while belonging allows for individuality, a process that requires awareness and is time consuming. Hundreds of thousands of children, now adults, never enjoyed being grandchildren, having been cheated out of a grandmother or two. Like blackened images on an MRI, these lesions alter their essence and presence. Now that they're becoming grandparents themselves, they discover how badly the deprivation and sorrow stings, retroactively. Teenagers can fight and argue with parents and can still find solace with grandparents, a safe place where they can air their grievances, get advice, and look forward to being pampered a little. Those who have grandmothers and grandfathers are very attached to them, by their kindheartedness, their magical ability to soothe and comfort without being judgmental.

The third generation connects well with the first. Kindred souls. After all, these kids' parents rebelled against their own parents and, now they, the third generation, rebel against their parents, the second generation, which brings them closer yet again to the first generation, their grandparents, and feel a sense of belonging, warmth and love for the grandparents in a way that they never felt toward their own parents, and just as they themselves will someday feel toward their own grandchildren.

In a dark cave a crack opens and warm light filters in.

At last, I connect the missing link for why I feel such a strong sense of belonging with Frieda.

THERE ARE DAYS LIKE THAT

Like an electrical short circuit, a power outage, or a battery going dead, suddenly the conductors and fluids disappear from my brain. I have no desire to go out and meet anyone. It's not even a matter of desire: after all, the disconnect simply shorts the circuit. My very being just wants to stay in neutral. Not ignite, not move, just be set there, just be in one place. It could be the joyful experience of writing or creating but, on the other hand, it could just as easily develop into a whole host of unpleasant thoughts such as:

- I'm not doing anything.
- Why am I dealing with rubbish?
- Why not get out of it right now?
- Why am I driven by the chaff rather than the wheat?
- Why am I losing important things, but find the silliest things?
- Should I begin/continue searching and, if so, why?
- Why is it that the very things I lose suddenly become as precious and vital as oxygen is to breathing?
- What's happening to my decision-making abilities?

The brain reports 'utter silence' and declares that there's no point in moving, it asks to remain in a state of nullification, of nothingness. When this mood persists, I don't want to leave my internal home. I don't want to move, but it's a temporary passivity and seemingly comfortable. I won't call anyone but, if they phone me, I'll react. A process might even begin of its own accord. And immediately I'll ask if it was really necessary to react. I've no reason or desire to move myself. It's a common occurrence: 'cruise control.' When the mood is low, it can be overcome by doing actions that require no thought.

It's best to do shopping when fatigue is great and the mood is low. This prevents wasting an alert mood on unimportant things, on routine matters, on the triviality of shopping, on what doesn't require any cognitive effort. It is reasonable to assume that when I buy bread, coffee or sugar, it may somewhat boost my mood. I leave alertness for, what are to me, sacred acts such as writing or painting.

Through these disconnects I connect with Frieda. But she shut herself off, through her obedience and her almost blind belief in the voice commanding her to go with everyone else to the neighborhood synagogue. This is where the disconnect, the severance, becomes empowered. The shutting off is a kind of protection and, simultaneously, denial, which can ward off madness.

BRAKE

Suddenly, as things near their end, everything comes to a halt. I'm not the one whose braking, something stronger than myself is stopping short, interrupting the experience in which I'm immersed. Things don't always get completed. The internal criticism is insufferable. In my eyes, things aren't good enough. I leave matters unfinished, setting the written pages aside in a drawer. Let them go through a period of ovulation and maturation in the dark, like plants in the nursery, protected by sheets of plastic. The spirit's brake pedal nips achievement in the bud, fends off praise, reins the will, leaves objects disorganized, untidy, leaves sorrows hung on the backs of chairs like clothes left to dry indefinitely, if not for eternity.

I find myself slamming on the brakes at the threshold of success. The soul's brake attempts to preempt continuity, realization, the joy of finishing, success. Does this derive from Frieda's unfinished life? Will her story ever come to fruition? What I wouldn't give for just one reader, who either stumbles over this book or is moved to read Frieda's story, to have heard something about her, about her birthplace, to contact me and add one single historic detail.

SUFFERING THAT BECOMES FERTILIZER, A NEW BEGINNING

One advantage of disconnecting and not wanting to leave your comfort zone is you're more inclined to use what is readily available at home. For example, soup or salad prepared from whatever is at hand is guaranteed to result in a unique taste. With a mindset of drawing a circle in the sand and staying only within its parameters there is a desire-fatigue, a disconnect, and we make use of whatever is accessible, what is closest in proximity to where we're standing. Mint grows in a nearby planter; in the adjacent pot, lemongrass. There's a fresh lemon winking at us on the countertop. Yesterday's stale bread isn't so terrible. Easily accessed ingredients save walking to the grocery and buying extraneous food items and other products. Keeping things such as boxes or containers in order not to waste money or, even more so, energy.

Inactivity, obeying commands, being a model citizen, having faith; all these lead Frieda and her neighbors to the point of no return. And we, the descendants, are left here with hacked-off roots and stumped trunks; the effort to continue growing branches comes at a high price. The outcome: slow, short growth, medium-sized fruit. The effort put into preserving the past combined with the effort to grow is exhausting. No one can discern this minuscule effort until fatigue takes over, in the midst of walking, trying to stand straight, as upright as possible. Meanwhile we walk, as long as we're able to. Surviving, but not always able to initiate. One of the screws are loose, or has gone missing.

The short circuits derive from the distance between the planet on which Frieda lives and the place where I live. Abba never told me a thing about the mass grave where his mother and family were buried. I discovered it myself many years later. The are no names of those who perished engraved on the mass grave and, therefore, there will always be a doubt and some uncertainty about their *denouement*, how and when they left this earth.

This lack of clarity is the inception of a work of art.

MELODY

Writing, just like a prayer or an internal melody, writes itself. By going back in time to Frieda, I dig deep into the origins of my identity. I begin to understand the source of my name and family history. Touching on the suffering, the silence, the tiny amount of information, something stronger than myself starts to sprout, to grow.

A plant needs aerated, not tamped down, earth in order for it to flourish. I needed to overcome Abba's decision to forego the name I should have been given, Ruth, since I was born precisely on the 6th Sivan in the Hebrew calendar, the date of the Festival of Shavuot when the Torah was given to the Jewish People and when the Book of Ruth is read. The Rabbi of the tiny synagogue on the corner of Hashmonaim and Yehuda HaLevi streets in Tel Aviv told my father that it is tradition to name children born on Shavuot 'Ruth' if it's a girl and 'Boaz' if it's a boy. However, Abba chose to name me, his firstborn daughter, after his mother. Nonetheless, Abba made sure to tell me about the Rabbi's suggestion.

Later on, I added the name Ruth as a middle name. Although I'm still called by my given name, I sign my artwork, photographs and paintings 'Aliza Ruth.' It took me years to adjust to the name Aliza, connoting both sorrow and joy. Now Bobbeh Frieda is like a comfy insole on an ill-fitting shoe. I bear her name like a weight but, the more

I delve into the name, the lighter it becomes.

I added the name Ruth because… if the Shoah had never happened… that would have been my name.

Alas the Shoah did happen, and impacted the lives of millions, among them tens of thousands of artists.

A FICTITIOUS DOWRY

In the paintings of Yosl Bergner, my neighbor when I was a child who remembered me taking accordion classes, kitchen utensils fly through the air. I imagine a grater, porcelain teacups, fragile drinking glasses set into metal rings with handles, a samovar, the embroidered tablecloth, bowls from which the scent of nostalgia wafts. Not only do I imagine the teacup but also the flow of conversation, its warm aroma, the stories my Bobbeh weaves in her dreams. I feel my spirit uplifted: someone grabs onto a tuft of my hair and gently pull me up. I feel the tickle of air in my body. Bobbeh disappeared but look! She's back! The dimensions of distance and time between us, that were stretched to infinity, to diametric poles, now take on a new meaning, of astonishing proximity.

We sit close, sipping tea from ornamental cups. My dress touches hers.

We listen to Maurice Ravel's 'Pavane for a Dead Princess.' What was Frieda's nature? That of a farmer? A lover of animals? A woman of culture? Nobility, the wife of a Rabbi, who appreciated fine music and literature? Her kitchen was simple, aside from a few porcelain dishes. Every so often she succumbed to temptation, in a sort of momentary madness, purchasing a few high-quality baking utensils and special teacups.

One very thin, fragile porcelain cup adorned with crimson roses remains orphaned on the table. Its shape is so delicate and so clear in my mind that I feel its warmth in my palms. Despite the distance I can taste the fine bone china on my tongue. Purple roses adorn a second, similar cup. Here I am, seated at a wooden table covered in the hieroglyphics of nicks and scratches, sipping tea alongside Frieda. She places bitter-sweet ginger snaps on the table, then tucks her colorful skirt in and asks me to come closer. Every time I drink from this beautiful cup, I'm reminded of how few mementos I have from Bobbeh Frieda's kitchen, wishing I had more.

No wonder I paint memories, a fictitious dowry.

With a purple pencil I draw a ladder, building memories and flying off with them to faraway lands, cities, homes, rooms, until I reach Frieda's kitchen, and there I stop.

BOBBEH FRIEDA'S LAST SHABBAT

Even though she felt she was running out of strength, Frieda baked a challah that was sweeter than ever. She prepared fish, boiled a soup, rolled little matzah balls - *kneidlach*, Lena's favorite - cooked the meat with spices just the way Haim liked it, and stewed prune compote, just the way her mother used to make.

Soon they would light the Shabbat candles. Normally the housework and preparations before welcoming in the Shabbat simultaneously excited and calmed her but, this day, she couldn't shake away her sadness. Haim is silent. Lena is tense.

"No," Frieda was thinking, "Lena has reasons to be wound as tight as a spring, not just because she's worried about Yanek."

The tension in the air was palpable. Frieda lights the candles and, suddenly, choking back tears and crushing the cotton handkerchief in her hands, she begins swaying to and fro, trying to restrain herself. Haim places a hand on her shoulder, makes the blessings over the wine and the challah.

Frieda stuffs the moist handkerchief into her apron pocket and wipes her tears with the apron.

"This time it's not because of the onion," Haim's thinking

as he breaks off portions of bread, dipping each into the saucer of salt, and playfully tosses one to each of the two women at the table with a sly grin, trying to lighten the mood.

Suddenly Lena stands and leaves the room. "I'll be back in a moment," she says in a throaty hush.

Haim wants to call to her, but Frieda shushes him. "Let her be."

Haim and Frieda eat quietly. Lena returns, sits down and moves her food around the plate.

"Eat something. You're pale," Frieda says.

Lena sighs. "I'm not hungry today."

Frieda wipes her hands on her apron again and again. The three of them finish the meal in silence.

"Usually the prune compote is sweet," Frieda thinks, taking a spoonful, "but this time it's bland."

"Today the compote tastes odd," Lena thinks as she leaves the table again and goes to the sink to wash her mouth. Haim crosses his arms and says nothing.

"Ok, I get it, I get it," Frieda tries to smile.

"Well, I don't understand anything anymore," says Haim as he stands. "Thank you for the meal," he says gently, and scurries off to find solace in his holy books.

KALEIDOSCOPE

A photo can indeed freeze a moment in time but cannot capture the three dimensional perfection; nor do films, paintings, music or even a diary. Moments as a whole are etched in our memories, the smells, the colors, a virtual 3D movie scorched into our brains.

At Frieda's next-door neighbors' garden, three white geese braggartly squawk, pacing the green grass, leaving their droppings behind them, their long necks jutting towards the gray skies. They stop for a moment, then pick up where they left off. Guarding their territory, they are simultaneously charming and terrorizing: as soon as a stranger tries to enter, they attack. The geese's pastoral appearance utterly contrasts with the amount of poop and stench they leave everywhere. Frieda doesn't mind it. Her love of animals makes up for all their poor behavior and habits. Frieda is on good terms with her neighbor so, after the hyndik is fed his Shabbat portion, she gives the neighbor's geese the leftovers.

I look through the kaleidoscope - the good life.

I take a walk around the place, on the path of love paved with geese, cows, a Lithuanian turkey and a day-dreaming goat.

A DAY, AS IF THERE'S NO TOMORROW

I'm overcome with a sense of vigilance mixed with anxiety, as though tomorrow will not be another day. I feel an urgency bordering on panic as I need to quickly finish, organize, buy, take, return, and see to dozens of things, as if today is the last day. As though there's no tomorrow. And all this is jumbled with the will to excel and perhaps even receive positive feedback.

In the body's cavity as well as the oral cavity, sounds have strong reverberations, like the echo of a dentist's drill. When the voice is loud and strong, that resonance is amplified a thousand-fold. Only recently, Frieda, when I met you through our story, yours and mine, did I become aware of my intense longing and how oppressive it is.

A SLIP OF GROUND

Ninety percent of Vandžiogala's residents had a strip of property where they could grow vegetables, two or three cows, four goats, a few ducks, geese, and some hens. Mina and Frieda would swap vegetables for fruit, eggs for a jug of milk, goat cheese for a loaf of bread. Sometimes one of them would go up the road to look for a few more eggs for the Shabbat cake in return for some ripe tomatoes. One of the husbands would lug a sack of potatoes off somewhere and return with a bottle of wine. All those everyday activities kept the neighbors so busy that they never felt the growing anti-Semitism, the war barreling towards them.

Vandžiogala's population was diverse. Some children were part of the Hashomer HaTza'ir Jewish youth movement, which followed a completely secular lifestyle. Others belonged to the Beitar movement, which was more traditional. And others studied in the kheider. Some older children went to a secular school but came to the kheider in the evenings to brush up on their Chumash, Gemara and Talmud. In the haberdashery both Yiddish and Lithuanian were spoken. Most Jews followed tradition, praying three times a day, singing *zemiras*, Jewish hymns chanted around the table at lunch on Shabbat and during Jewish holidays. When Shabbat ended, an hour after sundown, they said the Havdalah prayer, distinguishing the separation between the sabbath and the work week about to commence.

Vandžiogala 's Jewish population successfully blended religious life with agricultural life and lived peacefully alongside their non-Jewish neighbors.

THE BOX OF MAGIC TRICKS

Our small town has always been relatively calm. But lately, everyone says one thing or another, and I've become so tired of the rumors. Mina, my good friend, told me about her cousin, a Rabbi in Budapest, who was caught by Nazis. They grabbed him by the beard, dragging him and mocking him in front of passersby. After this happened to one of her own family members, Mina became restless. First, she tidied the whole house. Then she began packing. Next thing you know, one evening she suddenly announced she was sailing to America with her husband. They left the children with her sister. I'll miss Mina. Me, I'm not capable of taking that kind of initiative. Leaving Lena. In any case, Haim's busy with his work and lately even more folk come to the house seeking his advice. Lena's so excited to be with Yanek. I see how her cheeks flush pink with happiness.

Come what may, we can't leave, at least not for now.

In the evenings I go to sleep early, almost falling off my legs. I've never been so exhausted. I need a long, deep rest. I've run out of strength. In the past, I'd go and help neighbors, but now I do only what's necessary in the house and the garden. It reassures me that Yehezkel and Leon aren't here. And yet, my soul is split. When the family was together, especially on Shabbat eve when I lit the candles, I could feel the harmony and wholeness enter and fill our home. But now, without the boys, the family is severed. We don't hear nearly enough from them, but I'm sure they're managing, focusing on their studies and will soon receive their diplomas.

Haim does what needs to be done. He helps the neighbors, offers advice, recruits funds for the needy, but his face… it's not like it once was. His role as the Rabbi is expanding, especially lately… people, feeling helpless, come for guidance, they consult, and even when there's no simple answer he uses his well-grounded logic, helps as best he can by mustering all his wisdom, answers their questions and puts them at ease.

The streets have been empty lately. People stay at home. I don't know how much longer this situation can go on. The rumors, the whispers, relatives from America talking about what they heard on the news. Everybody sticks to their routines. The war is advancing. Is the war coming to its end? And there I go again, repeating my father's Yiddish phrase: *Iber a yahr, nisht ergerer*. None the worse for a year that's passed.

Pavel, the farmer who used to take the cow to pasture, has enlisted. So now I take the cow out, but stay close to home. We can feel the tension all around us. Lucky I've got the garden to care for. No matter what happens, the plants, the goat, the turkey, are always happy to see me. But at night under the feather quilt, Haim tosses and turns, the bed creaks, and I turn to the other side. When he turns back again I try to lie quietly, pretending to be asleep because I don't want him to worry. It's hard to fall asleep with so many disturbing thoughts and, all of a sudden, it's the middle of the night and I find that I'm totally awake, vigilant. Then by midday I'm so tired. After hearing about how the Budapest Rabbi was tortured I started to worry much more, especially for Haim. Those kinds of thoughts flood me. I hope our little town won't be harmed. It's like the little wooden box where Lena keeps her colored beads. When you open it, it plays music and a tiny ballerina in a pink dress begins to dance, spinning in front of the mirror and, when you hold it at a certain angle, suddenly there are two dancers spinning. That's how Vandžiogala is: teensy, barely anyone knows where it is and, when you look at its center it becomes doubly good. Which goes to prove that no one would want to harm it? Right?

IS THAT A DOVE ON YOUR SHOULDER?

Frieda, it's lovely to sense that you're looking my way every so often. I feel as though a gentle dove is perched on my shoulder; the dove coos and whispers, "write, write," and when I want to stop, the white dove pecks at me, nudging me. It's you, Frieda; at any minute you'll be tapping the letters on the keyboard with your wing; in any event, the writing flows far faster than my thoughts and I can't keep up with them. I'm so thrilled that you've connected with me and that through you I'm able to summon the inspiration I need to keep writing.

DUST AND SPIRIT

Like cranes, who have known for generations exactly when to take off for warmer climates and when to return, so longing attempts to cope with pain, spreading its wings to distant Lithuania, returning recharged by its sights and sounds. The spiritual charger compensates for the absence. The spirit rises, whispers from the cavity of a grave, seeking tranquility. I answered. I had no choice.

Midway through my life, I took on a mission: to arouse your spirit from its slumber, Bobbeh Frieda, to cradle you, hold you close, to finally give you a place to rest. The spirit and the matter have become muddled. Look, the calm spirit is now returning to where it belongs, laden with experiences.

"And the dust shall settle on the earth as it was, and the spirit shall return to God who granted it," (Ecclesiastes 12:7). Your dust, Frieda, has admittedly returned to a foreign land, but not in the usual way; and here we are, your troubled spirit emerges again beseeching me, the one who remains, the one who bears the memory chip.

"Understand our family. Take action; keep going; think; write. Only then, after all these years, will I be able to rest."

So said the spirit, and I answered like an echo.

"I'm in need of some serious rest. The thread that binds us is delicate yet undeniably strong; just like an umbilical cord, so full of life, it has fulfilled its purpose and can now fall away and dissolve naturally."

WAKING THE DEAD

Two angels, Gabriel and Michael, flutter down, land on my shoulders and begin conversing between themselves and, only later, turn to me. The truth is, I'm not surprised, I knew they'd come. Yesterday, while I sat watching the sea on the Tel Aviv coast, a rainbow danced across the sky, ignoring helicopters circling the air. A white light beamed from the gray clouds.

From the café's window overlooking the beach, it looks as if the sun and clouds are playing games. At first, I felt the strong sun singing my skin but soon it was completely concealed by a random gray cloud. The attentive waitress noticed the blinding light and lowered the shades. Some minutes later it became quite dark and she had to raise the shades again. I kept putting my sunglasses on and taking them off until the rain started falling, the sun and clouds playing nicely above the crashing waves.

HEAVY SHOULDERS

Returning home in the evening, I first caught the sound of beating wings and only then felt the weight on my shoulders. It didn't hurt, especially after a yoga class, just a pleasant fluttering. I took my jacket off but the weight on my shoulders remained. The two angels.

Having taken their positions, Gabriel, on my left, began to talk. "Remember how Frieda rose to heaven? I wonder whether she predicted her end and that's why she wore her white synagogue dress or if it was pure coincidence."

Michael, on my right, countered, "There's no such thing as coincidence. You yourself taught me that there's a covert order to everything."

"Her life was short, but she knew how to use her time wisely, carefully measuring her hours and steps as she walked about her little garden; it meant so much to her."

"Indeed... she worked the land, fed the animals, cleaned up, all very peacefully, methodically, as though plowing her way through the great seas."

"Whatever she needed, all the treasures in this world were there in her little garden; she didn't need much to be satisfied."

"Unlike others, she lacked for nothing. And even shared. Such a righteous woman."

"The truth is, she didn't deserve such an end. Not that

anyone does but, what can you do, those, too, rise quickly to heaven."

"The hardest moment was separating the three…"

"Yes, Frieda, Haim and Lena held hands so tightly."

"Come to think of it, why are we still contending with this old matter? Who keeps bringing it up?"

"It's she who's harping on it, as though eighty years haven't passed."

"She's the one raising the dead?"

"Their lives were short whereas their deaths have lengthened."

"After all, no one said their farewells to them. No funeral. No yahrzeit. No anniversary of death."

"And, like Frieda, look how the granddaughter dotes not only on people but on the cow, the goat, the turkey."

"Animals rise to heaven, too, but to a more distanced place; anyway, that's not our concern, animals are the Archangel Fhelyai's responsibility."

"He had too much on his plate, after all, there were so many animals! The cow, the white goat, the tall turkey."

"Perhaps the time's come to stop raising the dead?" Gabriel asked.

I never heard an answer. A fierce wind began to blow, rattling flakes of hail loudly against the windows. Did the cold drive the angels away? The weight on my shoulders lifted and I felt lighter; suddenly, I stopped writing. I stared out the window and, with perfect timing - two green parrots landed on the pecan tree.

A new morning.

Pink clouds played hide and seek with their gray space-mates.

The sun turned the sky a pale yellow, save for a few fluffy white clouds.

A cloud's lifespan is a mere half hour.

COGITO ERGO SUM

What did René Descartes mean when he proposed 'Cogito ergo sum,' I think, therefore I am?

Sometimes there's so much *Cogito* going on, and so little *sum*. So much thinking, so little being.

We could say: I don't think, therefore I am.

We could say: I am loved, therefore I am.

I have grandparents, therefore I am.

Abba speaks, therefore I am.

If only Bobbeh Frieda would sit me on her lap.

If only Abba would look deep into my eyes, tell me of those days and stroke my cheek, I'd be even more.

Being is existence, determination, resilience, the ability to kick back, to develop charisma.

Fear paralyzes and causes a person to become anonymous, a shadow, to walk slinking close to the walls, not make any noise, not draw unnecessary attention, do everything on their own, never ask for help. Fear leads to avoidance, the polar opposite of presence. If only Abba had not just survived, but had truly existed and was present, my being might have taken shape and become empowered already in early childhood.

WHAT IS LEFT UNSAID CAN'T BE REGRETTED

Although there are more than six million mourning and suffering the loss of those who perished in the Shoah, bereavement remains a very private affair.

Even after I understood, only a few years ago, the degree to which I belong to that hurting Second Generation, I have steered clear of ceremonies, conferences, meetings, and anything even remotely related to lighting torches or Holocaust Remembrance Day. The two times I did attend such events, I met several people who were more than eager to voice their stories, even more than to listen, along with those active in ensuring Shoah commemoration continue. Once, when my paintings were being shown in an exhibit at a particular community center, there was a Shoah memorial going on. It was there that I witnessed the urgency, the importance of positioning, the politics, the glorification of that second generation, progeny of the partisans, as compared to others. I chose to focus on the image of my Bobbeh, silent in the name of silent millions.

Like the others whose mouths were shut closed, I opted for the hallowed ritual of a one-woman ceremony, a liturgy for one woman writing about another. After my Bobbeh began answering me, I wrote to her directly, which filled us both with extraordinary bliss. I write on behalf of my family who no longer is, and Frieda answers on behalf of the dead. Frieda and I chose a mode of mute communication.

ZIKARON BA'SALON: MEMORIALIZING IN THE LIVING ROOM

I remember a friend and I decided I'd relate my family's narrative to a gathering of friends to be held in her living room. The atmosphere was both intimate and accepting. Over the years the concept of *Zikaron ba'Salon* took shape in the town of Hod Hasharon. Every time I agreed to share my family's story, I'd tell it in a different way. And again, I'd hear from attendees what their own families went through in the Diaspora: the cruelty, the loss, the never-ending search.

TEXTBOOK-PERFECT CHILDREN

And it shall be in the end times that tranquility shall come down upon all.

The Shoah will seem so distant that it will no longer connect to us.

Our fears and worries will be erased. We shall not be so concerned, nor feel guilt.

We shall rise come morning with a song in our heart, feel at ease, everything will be so simple, as it is for those who are not second generation and thus do not carry an old pain.

Then we will no longer strive to be textbook-perfect children.

ON THE WAY TO SYNAGOGUE

It is Shabbat morning. Haim and Yehezkel, dressed in Shabbat clothes, are the first to set out and walk to the *shul*, the synagogue, chatting quietly as they go. Once they arrive, several worshippers greet them warmly. Haim takes off his hat. Drops of dew tip from the brim. He hangs the hat on the rack and smooths his *tallit*. Frieda and Leon are waiting for Lena who's dithering over whether to wear the floral dress or the monochromatic one. She carefully chooses perfectly suited stockings, then smiles broadly upon seeing her reflection in the mirror.

Frieda urges Lena to hurry. Lena skips in delight, excited in her Shabbat finery. They set out, passing neighbors' homes in their modest neighborhood. Women wear festive clothing, grip the hands of their little children, nod in greeting to each other. They hurry to get to shul on time. As they remove their heavy coats and hang them in the shul's foyer, the warmth of the communal gathering is palpable. As soon as they step inside, the light snow turns into a blizzard.

"What luck!" Frieda whispers to Lena. "We've come right on time. He who sits on high waited until we entered!"

Lena smiles and squeezes her mother's hand.

The chanting of prayer silences the chatterers and unites the congregation. During the week that passed, each was busy with her or his life and now, here they all are, humming and singing Shabbat prayers in unison. The women peek at each other's dresses, discern a young woman's rounded belly, smile at how the children are growing taller, detect one's whitening hair peeking out from under her headscarf; and another's wrinkles, her smile actually accentuates the change. A thread of worry has woven its way into the prayers of late but the power of singing placates the spirit.

LITHUANIANS ARE CRUELER THAN NAZIS. Is that even possible?

With the German army's invasion of the USSR on 22 June 1941, known as the Barbarossa Operation, some Jews from Vandžiogala, especially the younger ones, attempted to flee to Russia via Latvia. Some were murdered by local Lithuanian nationalists who ambushed them. The bulk were forced to return because the Germans had gotten there first. On 25 June 1941, the Germans entered Vandžiogala and immediately imposed restrictions on the Jews, such as the mandate requiring that they wear a yellow patch and prohibiting Jews from using sidewalks. Local Lithuanians helped the Germans locate Jewish homes and mark them with the word 'Jude.'

Jews, both men and women, were forced into harsh humiliating labor in their Lithuanian neighbors' homes and farms, such as cleaning outhouses, etc. Some Jews were taken to do farmwork in estates in the adjacent town of Labanoras.

On 8 July 1941, armed Lithuanians arrested 68 Jewish boys and brought them to the neighborhood of Borekas near the Jewish cemetery. They forced them to remove their clothes and shoes, were ordered to dig pits, and the murderers shot them all. The remaining Jews were herded into a kind of ghetto at the end of Keidan Street. Their belongings and possessions were stolen by the Lithuanians.

On Shabbat, 16th of the month of Av, year 5701 on the Jewish calendar (9 August 1941), although some claim it was actually a week later, the shul was surrounded by dozens of armed Lithuanians while the Jews were praying inside. Some one hundred people, including the elderly **Rabbi Haim Klebanov**, were pulled out of the synagogue and loaded onto wagons. They were joined by several women. The wagons were led to the township of Babtai, twelve kilometers from Vandžiogala, where they were held for some two weeks in the town's synagogue until they were all executed.

On August 28th, the remaining Jews were gathered in the town's market square: women, children, men, elderly, and those meanwhile caught in hiding places in nearby locations. All were brought to Babtai and shot in the same place where the others had been shot. Some women expressed opposition. They were shot in their lower limbs and buried while still alive. From Vandžiogala 's entire Jewish population less than 10 Jews survived. Several reached the Kovno Ghetto and from there fled before the extermination or joined the partisans.

Locals turned the Vandžiogala synagogue into a cowshed. They smashed all the gravestones in the Jewish cemetery and used the pieces to pave the paths adjacent to their homes.

From the Registrar of Communities, Lithuania. Edited by Dov Levin

MATHEMATICS DOES NOT CAUSE BURNS

Compared to the seemingly non-committal passive verb 'perished,' verbs such as humiliated, robbed, looted, shot, strangled, murdered, slaughtered, and buried alive convey an image that defies logic and is deeply traumatic.

But who in those days had time to deal with traumas? Who thought of therapy back them? Who even had the option to receive treatment? Too many understood this too late.

Dry hard facts: Lithuania has the highest percentage of murdered Jews among all Jewish communities exterminated in the Holocaust.

There's no point calculating what percentage three people from my family account for among the 212,000 Lithuanian Jews who perished by outright murder in the Holocaust. Total number of Lithuanian Jews before the Shoah: 220,000.

Millions perished in the Shoah, yet the numbers slip beneath our radar, or glide above our heads. Some of us display apathy until… until they are personally burnt, until a crevice cracks wide opens. At first, you can barely see it; then it becomes a dull pain; sometimes that can take years.

A break or fracture in the heart is very different from a crack in a vessel. The vessel does not suffer.

A glimmer of light beaming through a gap is a hopeful metaphor, a poetic illusion, transient.

In Leonard Cohen's 'Anthem,' he sings "There is a crack in everything. That's how the light gets in," inspired from the words of Rabbi Nachman of Breslau (1772-1810), founder of a Hassidic dynasty.

Most of us are born to carry on a legacy: despite the sorrow, when the shivah the Jewish custom of mourning the deceased for seven days, comes to a close, we are expected to get up and look ahead to the future, towards rectification, towards the light.

KINTSUGI: FILLING CRACKS WITH GOLD

Although Ecclesiastes 1:15 states that some things cannot be fixed, that "that which is crooked cannot be made straight," repairs can take on many forms, such as patchwork, shoes repair, tikkun olam, repairing the world, bioarcheology and remedies.

Kintsugi is the Japanese art of putting broken pottery pieces back together by filling the cracks with gold - a metaphor for embracing your flaws and imperfections. Artists view the crack and its repair as part of the vessel's history, its nature, its appearance. The art of kintsugi is inextricably linked to the Japanese philosophy of wabi-sabi: a worldview centered on the acceptance of transience, imperfection and the beauty found in simplicity, values the old, the scratched and rusted, bestowing beauty and power on cracks and fissures. In other words, scars are not something to hide, rather to take pride in.

***

*For me, the process of creating and of writing infuses
a flow of energy
Into that which is broken but,
Instead of filling the fractures with liquid gold,
I breathe new life into them by means of words.
Into the pit, the spaces, the slits, the cracks.
Without this energy-charged gold
How can I contain the vastness of all that is going on?
The lines above testify to the bore, the gap that has
been pried open.
Even the truth of what occurred in the town's history
is hazy.
I build a story link by link.*

AN ITALIAN JOKE AND METAPHOR

In the Italian film 'Kaos,' the protagonist shapes a giant storage jar, an amphora, from links and links of clay. His handiwork can only be completed if he enters into the jug's base and works on the internal walls from there. However, so focused on his endeavor the hero discovers, to his shock, that he has not left himself an exit and remains imprisoned in the jug.

I must be cautious not to, God forbid, lose focus while writing and get stuck in 1941 Lithuania, having traveled back in time to that dark period. I must continue writing and polishing and, finally, to complete the work of editing and publishing, and come out the other end of the tunnel towards the light, to the now, to today.

LULLABY FOR THE DECEASED

Darkness has fallen. Good night, Frieda. If I could sing you one song before you closed your eyes, it would be the wonderful lullaby you sung to your children.

"Close your eyes and summon... a special dream

Think of, for example... a golden peacock

When you fall asleep, the peacock will fly to your bed, perch on the armchair

Bow its crowned head and fan out his magnificent train

Displaying his iridescent tail feathers, each with its own purple eye

And then slowly, slowly the eyes shut."

***

Then I'd stand next to the dead others: Zeideh, Lena, the neighbors, and sing to them too.

"Summon for yourselves ... a special dream

Think of, for example... a golden peacock

When you fall asleep, the peacock will fly to your bed, perch on the armchair

Bow its crowned head and fan out his magnificent train

Displaying his iridescent tail feathers, each with its own purple eye

And then slowly, slowly peace will be upon you."

EPILOGUE IN LIEU OF KADDISH

Cock-a-doodle-doo! Gob-gob-gobble! It's me again, the turkey, my word is my bond. And I'll keep my promise to offer closing remarks. However, this is not a summary as not everything can be summed up. It's not exactly *Kaddish*, the mourner's prayer, either, for the Jews community would have whispered of strangers like me, "*Nisht fon unzereh*," not one of ours, and really, I'm not one of them, but I lived among them, in their home and, even more than it being a good deed to say some closing words, I feel the need to do so.

I never tasted *imberlakh*, though I heard so much about the strange, tangy Lithuanian treat. Ginger is not my favorite grain. Over the years I became an *alteh kopf*, a wise old thing, even if my wisdom was only as great as a birdbrain can manage. But I saw some things, acquired experience. And the truth is, I didn't understand everything, although what I did sniff out and taste, may the Almighty take mercy, no words can begin to describe.

A FEATHER, A JEST

Being the one to bring this narrative to a close, I'll end with a smile. Perhaps it's no more than a desperate attempt at clownishness. My feathers, after they're plucked, are cleaned and dipped in ink. They are quills for scribes who write the Torah and other religious documents. They are pens for wise men. And here I am tying up the ends of Frieda's story without a feather, and that is no joke.

What remains, and with this I shall end, is a sense of humor. The Lithuanian Jews were very serious, probing deep into whatever they were doing. But sometimes (my right wing to God I can't understand the phenomenon) when it came to humor, they were the first to laugh, yes, even at themselves, rising above the situation. They would cry and then suddenly break into peals of laughter, and sometimes cry while they were doubled over with laughter. Their laughter was contagious and, like everything they did, they laughed thoroughly, and those who laughs last laugh best. Sadly, that's me.

WINGLESS CREATURES

The excitement I felt as the trip to Lithuania approached felt different from any I've experienced. I am not going to visit a particular person or a specific address. I'm going to the place Abba wasn't capable of visiting. I'm going in order to open a window onto his native land, a Lithuanian window that was slammed shut on his bleeding fingers.

Now, with the number of years ahead of me far shorter than the number of years I've lived, I look towards the past. Precisely now, when the load my back has borne lightens as the bones weaken, the value I place on any given moment grows. The bones become lighter, but the moments become heavier.

In the archives of the Association of Lithuanian Jews in Israel there are no documents relating to my family. I feel like the daughter of divorced parents. My mother: The Association for the Jews from Vilna; my father: The Association for the Jews from Lithuania. Even the volunteer at the Association of Lithuanian Jews in Israel wondered why the organization was split in two.

What would Abba say of my investigative research and journey? My father never agreed to return to that scorched earth.

And I am searching for diamonds among the coal ash.

IMAGINATION VS. REALITY

After the hyndik signed off, something happened.

The trip to Lithuania transpired. The grayed image became tangible, and disturbing.

For the sake of remembrance, all that I had imagined couldn't come close to the horror.

In my imagination, Zeideh and his family perished in the synagogue, but that's not necessarily fact. They were led from the synagogue to the forest. There, they dug a massive pit, and there, right next to the town, they were murdered. The corpses were flung into the vast pit.

I walked through that forest, silent, sinking into the mud. I visited the mass grave.

I was silent, with them.

MY FATHER FORGOT HOW TO HUG

Years pass, and I see things differently.

Having no other choice, Abba's way of overcoming the past was to get an excellent education, understand the culture, to carry himself with determination and elegance and season with a sprinkling of dry humor. Above it all hovered a puffy little cloud of silence.

Silence was power.

Abba shared very little about his parents and sister, stashing away vital links in the generational chain in a secret hiding place where they can't be found. By writing, I filled in the blanks, creating my own links, one by one, and now I join the elusive, invisible links to create a unique necklace, an original.

DISAPPOINTMENT DOESN'T GET A SEAT AT THE TABLE

An empty chair is earmarked for hope, which hopefully will arrive soon.

An empty chair is set aside for the prophet, the messiah, for salvation, which will arrive soon.

We long for mother, for father, for a sister to return.

No chair is set aside for disappointment. It hasn't been invited, so no one is waiting for it.

And when disappointment comes, we have no option other than to accept it, the way we accept thunder, a flood, bad news, shock.

It's called 'overcoming' and, in fact, as the years pass, we learn to live with absence.

ABBA'S WAY OF STAYING ALIVE

Did the name Yehezkel infuse him with stamina? In Hebrew, his name means 'God strengthens.'

Abba, an outline, remains the contour of my father.

Abba invented the reduction method. "Do you remember what you wore last year?" he'd ask when I wanted a new item of clothing.

The war made him stern. His brain held countless insights, but his heart wore a thick shell of armor.

Abba was like a turtle on the verge of extinction, occasionally poking its head out.

Yes, Abba was deeply moved by the artistry of photography, formulae, the moisturizers and face creams he produced, but mostly he stayed well inside his protective shell.

Moments of pleasure for Abba: working, studying, photography, writing with a fountain pen, a handful of friends, jokes and a swill of liquor, preferably French.

In the living room, which at night doubled as bedroom, was a wooden bookshelf with drawers and cabinets. One of the doors, when opened downward, would flick on an internal switch and light up the hidden mini-bar, an alcove lined with mirrors, doubling the bottles of liqueur, Calvados brandy, Cointreau. A few wine glasses bid their time until an important guest would visit and that little cupboard would be opened. It was like a clandestine weapons trove but, in this case, a stash for the little joys in life, long-ago memories of better times, of *La Belle Époque* in France before that war.

Abba rarely sipped an alcoholic drink even at celebrations. For the most part, he was a practical and industrious man.

In our home, the short corridor leading to the bathroom held a small niche which hid a narrow, well-organized wooden cabinet holding work tools. The door's inner panel was sketched with outlines of a screwdriver, plier, hammer, the items perfectly arranged. A specific item not in its place would be instantly identified by its empty contour.

The silhouettes of Abba's parents and sister remained as empty as shadows.

Abba never allowed himself to become immersed in sorrow. He hurried onwards, *weiter*, to work, to organize, to photograph, to repair.

From time to time, after removing the roll of film from the belly of the camera, whether the Zorki or the Leica which he truly loved, he would head for 'Amilani,' the film developing store on Sheinkin Street in 1960s Tel Aviv, excitedly hand the roll over, and return to collect the black and white photos.

Abba was the family photographer. Truly, an artist. Following in his footsteps, I also take photos. I set up a darkroom in the bomb shelter where I could develop negatives and produce printed photos, even retouching with Kodak colors. To this day I enjoy infusing monochrome with color.

Abba held himself very straight when he walked, erect as though he was dancing, clad in his suit and tie, occasionally looking like a Parisian in Tel Aviv's suffocating heat. He bought his custom made Borsellino's in the hat store on

Sheinkin Street, wearing it tugged down at an elegant angle. But unlike Humphrey Bogart, from under the rim of his hat Abba's charming smile revealed nothing. Who could have begun to imagine, judging by his noble demeanor, what he'd experienced, how tense he always was, or the breadth of his knowledge?

Among the books Abba read, in addition to professional literature, were Chekov, Gogol, Sholokhov, Kafka, and many more, in their original languages. At high school parent and teacher meetings he chatted in Russian with Mrs. Levinson, my scary chemistry teacher. But despite his education and intellectual depth and insight, he was never able to comprehend how his family, his hometown, and its entire Jewish population were erased in a single moment. Who can possibly absorb such a thing?

Imagine this: you leave your house, the front door key in your pocket, but you have nothing to come back to; everything you've known has disappeared, obliterated, like a roll of film pulled from the camera's gut and accidentally exposed to full sunlight. Think of Fellini's 'Roma' where the light causes all the paintings to fade and disappear.

The current war in Ukraine offers me another perspective on Abba, reminding me of what happens when, all at once, normal daily life disappears… and you become a refugee.

THE KEY

As was her wont, every morning she'd clear the table,
drink coffee, empty the dishwasher, speak with a friend.
Normally, every Wednesday she'd put on a leotard,
rush to Pilates class, shop online
and later, usually, work from home,
speak with the boss on Zoom,
make dinner, put her son to bed,
and, after dark, she'd normally kick back
on the green recliner with a sigh and only
then watch something on TV.
But now, after the shelling, she took off her bra,
put on a soft t-shirt and coat,
stuffed a scarf and blanket into a backpack,
woke her son, struggled to answer his questions,
and locked the door
leaving their home, quite unusually, she
didn't slip the key under the doormat.
holding tight to her son's small hand
which, quite unusual for him, squeezes hers with all his might,
they now walk in a long convoy toward the border.
and, quite unlike her, she doesn't look back.
A day has passed and she hasn't heard from her husband
who left their home in the middle of the night,
cellphone screen going dark, battery running down,
burning smell of soot and dust in the air,
the door key orphaned in her coat pocket.
She squeezes it so tight that it splits open her skin.

***

Despite everything he'd been through, Abba was a very good father. He was an emulation-worthy example of wisdom, a polyglot, musically inclined, modest but, in 1941, his emotionality was locked in a safe.

Abba passed from this world with his untold stories intact. He wasn't one to compliment. He forgot how to hug.

A VIGILANT SECOND GENERATION

After the bearers of numbers on their forearms have passed away, gone forever, it is we who are left, the Second Generation, triggered, fraught, sorrow tattooed onto the chambers of our hearts.

Actually, those of my generation born in Israel as WWII subsided almost immediately encountered Israel's 1948 War of Independence. A country was rising on its feet, steadying itself, and an entire generation lived modestly in a framework of rationing formally titled 'The Austerity.' Parents worked, a troubled generation who forgot to show warmth, to compliment, to hug, because they themselves hadn't experienced that hug.

And, as war is war, there are unwritten rules; primarily, it's about surviving, being tough, being vigilant, being efficient, and keeping emotions well-hidden in some back drawer.

As the years passed I discovered the scope of the burden placed on my shoulders. I woke up one day realizing that I, too, belong to that Second Generation.

It's no simple thing to be Second Generation Holocaust Survivors. It's an equation missing one variable. We felt something dark, important, but intangible lurking in the air; we are the descendants of murky visions of grandparents:

we breathe chilly air. We are constantly on the alert. We are highly complex creatures. A protective vest imprisons our hearts. We are the children of war. Our cries are choked. Our joy locked up, the key thrown away.

On occasion, just briefly, we break through the prison of the self. We weren't told anything… but we knew. With the best of intentions, they wanted to wrap us in cotton wool, but it turned into some kind of jail; we weren't even aware of being comfortably incarcerated.

Sometimes, suddenly and without warning, a window of honesty and authentic joy flew open.

How does the window open? Where is the key hidden? We have no idea.

It was a window of opportunity but the window was soon slammed shut. We want it to reopen, desperate to feel the warmth, both of ourselves and our loved one. But the window was locked.

Once again there's a puzzle with a piece missing.

We're like clerks hurrying to shut the little service window which has just been opened to avoid being bothered with questions, requests, demands and stares.

The clerk wishes to prevent the threat of closeness and scrupulous eyes.

Just leave the poor clerk in peace and quiet.

In retrospect, my generation has everything it needs, but something element has been irretrievably misplaced, perhaps inadvertently kicked under the grandfather clock? The box? The main puzzle piece? The instruction manual? Perhaps not. All the pieces are there. So what's missing? The love of the game? In vain we seek that one missing variable, that cotter pin not released.

And the more we search, the more the variables multiply.

We are creatures burdened by layers to the point where each layer seems to have its own personality and character traits: dozens of matryoshkas set one inside the other.

God, what's this vigilance? Even when we complete our tasks, we're left all wound up; someone forgot to open our safety hatch.

***

"What have we done? Are we truly guilty?" these wingless creatures ask. The layers which have gripped and encompassed them, suddenly and without warning, begin to move and force all the creatures' vitality inwards. Like cars in a junkyard. There's no air. No oxygen. Only great fatigue. And it really is cold.

Midsummer, a yolk-yellow sun and, despite so many people around, loneliness.

What is troubling us? Have a Zeideh, Bobbeh, aunt, uncle, been lost forever?

We are lost souls running after lost time.

We were promised a technicolor movie but it's all in black and white.

We were promised a movie with sound but we're walking around in a silent film.

We are the 'everything's fine' children, even though most of us are on guard, ready to pounce.

The influence of the war that just ended in Europe seeped into the wars of Israel, the women whose husbands spent months on reserve duty, the mothers left home with the children. We're always wary. The past pours into the present and is already knocking on the futures of the next generation.

It would have all been different if not for the Holocaust, if Bobbeh Frieda would have hugged me, if Zeideh Haim would have stroked my head and comforted me, if Lena would have told me how the house looked, what it's like being a teacher, and how pretty Lithuania is.

***

What remains are some simple letters, the last letters written by Lena, my aunt, my father's sister, laying in a drawer and eventually translated. They are steeped in longing for her brother. Lena notes that their parents' greatest joy is receiving letters from the boys. Lena's letters from Lithuania suddenly stopped coming, quashing the brothers' hopes and happiness.

LITHUANIANS, SO THEY SAY, REALLY DO LOVE THEIR ANIMALS

Forest. Look how much forest there is! You actually can see the forest for the trees. In the Register of Communities, the murder of six hundred Jews from two towns is laconically described. The closer my departure date with the Lithuania delegation approached, the more I began to comprehend that they weren't murdered in the shul.

The Lithuanians of the time were a very wily people: had the Jews been killed in the synagogue, not only would the gunshots have been heard but the Lithuanians would have needed to transport hundreds of corpses to some other location. It would be far more efficient to carry out the murders, and preserve the huge secret, if the six hundred Jews gathered in the shul were led to the forest. I went there in search of a mass grave. It's barely possible to find the monument.

A thick, deep forest which, between its leaves and branches, conceals the long convoy. A forest of tall upright trunks hears the screams, the moans, the cries. Its roots hear commands in Lithuanian, hear the echo of gunshots. Every single person in the convoy: women, children and men, led and halted; realizing, fearing, praying; shot, collapsed and crumpled, without a speck of mercy, at the brink of the pit they dug. First those tree trunks heard hundreds of voices but, as the night's hours passed, the sounds were muffled and the trunks felt the shaking and shuddering of their roots.

The further into their mission, the more streamlined the Lithuanians became. Half the pit, already filled with still-warm bodies, was covered over by a handful of Jews who, after all they'd seen and experienced, viewed themselves as already dead. Silvery pearls of tears twinkled on their shovels in the stars' white light, and spilled onto the heaped corpses. A dozen. Another dozen. Shot, pitched into the great pit. The Jews saved the Lithuanians the work of digging and covering over. Standing off to the side, one Lithuanian was smoking, another stroked his dog, a third walked off a little way to urinate as he whistled the Lithuanian anthem.

The pit's final layer was covered almost entirely by Rabbi Haim, who watched how six hundred cherished fellow Jews, among them his wife, daughter and his congregation, believers, neighbors, some of whom believed a little less, lay in organized rows, because the Lithuanians were highly methodical. Haim would sneak glances at his wife Frieda through the kheider window while she skillfully hoed the garden next to their small home. Haim, however, with his hands unskilled, slowly covered the pit as the Lithuanians mocked his lack of expertise and urged him to work faster.

He was cold. Like the others, he was forced to strip down, his white beard trembling against the pale skin of a body that had known sixty years of love, learning and teaching. The house key was in the pocket of his trousers. Why had he taken it today of all days rather than hide it in its usual spot? It gave him great satisfaction to know that his two sons were not in Lithuania. But the three of them: he, his wife and daughter, had left the shul together, a harnessed cart waiting to take them to the nearby town of Babtai.

"Haim, take the key with you today. Put it deep in your pocket," said Frieda, whose heightened sense of premonition drove her words. And he, who'd studied thousands of pages of Talmud, nodded and didn't ask why, as he might have done on any other occasion because he, too, knew in his own way what had not been expressly worded. Frieda didn't laugh as she usually did, "Haim, you always ask questions. You're a true Litvak, believe me. The goat whispers it's so, the turkey gobbles it's so, and even the stars light up that which is concealed and not written in the books."

Suddenly Haim is shaken out of his thoughts. A young, bull-necked Lithuanian heard the tinkle of the key falling and screeched. "Bend down, Mr. Naked with the beard of a goat, give it to me or I'll break your neck… well, at least I won't have to break the door down if I have the key, which will save me having to get it repaired. No, don't give me the address; everyone knows which is the Rabbi's home. Don't worry, you old, wrinkled thing, I'll take really good care of it, of the house. You can rest assured…"

The Lithuanian winked at his friends in the darkness. Like his father and grandfather and all the Klebanov family, Haim did not shed a tear, nor did he sigh. No one knew what was going through his mind, if anything could go through someone's mind at such a time. The silence and the cold enveloped Haim like the lidded silver box that housed the *etrog* on Sukkot. He felt that this coming Rosh Hashana there'd be no one to bless, no one he could greet with, "A sweet new year."

The cold began to penetrate his bones. Earlier, the Lithuanians had prepared a bonfire to keep their hands, agonized from their hard work, warm. The blistered thumbs and first fingers hurt so badly from having to pull the trigger so many times. Into the bonfire's shooting colors they tossed leather shoes, socks, clothes, prayer shawls. They found it intriguing that the smaller items of clothing sparked so quickly. An odd sound of writhing and a terrible smell rose from the bonfire. Igor the dog, circling the bonfire at a safe distance, was confused as to what was happening on this strange night.

Haim was longing to lie down among his friends, among the clumps of earth which, in late August, were relatively warm. Lena lay somewhere beneath his bare feet. His right foot came across her big toe which, over the course of the past year, had begun to bend as though it wished to connect with the other four more closely. His thoughts went back in time: yes, it was here, precisely, where his children had gathered mushrooms emerging from this fertile soil.

Lithuanians were screaming. He recognized some of the voices. Haim covered the rest of the pit almost entirely, leaving a narrow rectangle. As he heard the shot ring out, he was thinking how lucky he was that his two sons were studying in France and how, even though they were clever and smart, they could never have begun to imagine the bitter end to which their father, mother and sister had come. The two were studying sciences: chemical engineering and electrical engineering, and were highly proficient in calculating complex formulae in their adopted French language. They, at least, would wish each other a sweet new year.

And Haim thought about the key and how it had always been hidden near the back entrance in the white milk pail with its rusting blue lip, the pail that Frieda always described as a blend of heaven and earth and never wanted to replace because every scratch and every streak of rust that took shape over time seemed to her like a developing impressionist painting. Those were Haim's thoughts. and he thought about the backs of her aching knees which also bore markings, a kind of delicate blue embroidery. For a moment, out of habit of looking skywards to check when Shabbat was over, Haim detected through the treetops, three stars, thirty stars, hundreds of stars of the fiercest hue. This summer night was at its peak: a night worthy of a grand ball, he thought. He hoped his two sons had enjoyed at least one memorable night in the City of Lights; after all, they worked in the mornings, studied in the evenings and shut the lights off before they collapsed into a deep sleep, and… he collapsed perfectly into the place intended for him, because the Lithuanians are so incredibly shrewd. And he managed to whisper "*El maleh rahamim*…" God who is merciful. God who…

And a terrible smile touched his lips.

And all that remained for one of the gun toting soldiers was to cover and fill in the small rectangular space into which Haim fell, although his name, meaning life, given by his father, and his faith in God, did not save him in the end.

Thus Haim, my Zeideh, joined the dead.

I was never privileged to see him or to see, even for a moment, Frieda and Lena.

***

After the screaming, a tangible silence filled the forest, the bonfire died down into a red eye like that of a doom-spreading witch watching in the blackness, watching what was, what no longer is, because not even history's pages could record the silence that no one heard due to contriving Lithuanian efficiency. The forest, which all knew so closely, stands to this day not far from Kovno, still hiding the echoes and shadows of those events so utterly.

Thus, their backs facing the great pit, the six riflemen pissed on the bonfire's dying gasps. Then, chattering among themselves about another day's work done, they marched on. One of them could feel the metallic chill of the Rabbi's key in his pocket. The Rabbi's name didn't interest him an iota but the metal's coolness eased the pain of his trigger finger a little. Through his warped mind a thought slipped: it would be so easy to appropriate the Rabbi's little house, especially since the soldier's girlfriend was pregnant and had already asked about their shared future.

Turning towards Vandžiogala and Babtai, one of the soldiers spoke. "We did good work tonight, friends. A pity we don't have much time left to sleep. That damn bonfire. It took so long to put out."

Another spoke. "I've got a bottle of vodka in my pocket. Now's the time to celebrate, friends."

As they approached the towns in which not a single Jew remained, they sipped the rest of the vodka and tossed the bottle away. It shattered against a tree trunk.

One of the soldiers laughed raucously. "Actually, after a filthy night like this one, we deserved that vodka. We did an excellent job. Even more professional than the commander's instructions. Thank goodness we're rid of those vermin."

Then he glanced down. "What a shame though that my boots are filthy with mud." Then he bent a little to stroke the copper-furred dog trotting alongside them. Licking his owner's hurting hand, the dog sniffed at the boots and began to move faster, wagging his tail and listening carefully to the tone his master spoke in as the soldier patted his back.

"Well, Igor, what a night it was. See, Igor? The stars are getting paler and dawn is almost here. We'll all be able to lie down soon. We're dead beat exhausted, right, my lovely doggie?"

Lithuanians, so they say, really do love their animals.

THREE POSTCARDS FROM LENA

Translation of a postcard sent to Perpignan in southern France, stamped with a swastika:

Via Romainel. Vilnius*,
21 November 1940

MY DEAR, DELIGHTFUL BROTHER,

I received your postcard yesterday. You cannot imagine how happy I am today. I couldn't believe my eyes when I saw it was from you, I just wish you could have written more.

Even though I'm sure our parents also received a postcard, I've just informed them of the contents of yours.

You cannot imagine what joy it brings them, and it seems they also wrote to you. Just wait, you'll see that our parents are healthy and think of you all the time. As for me, don't be sad. As you know from the telegram, I'm working at Vilna's governmental high school number 12.

I've been working since the start of this school year, 16 September. I teach grades 5, 6 and 7. I'm very satisfied with my work, and they're satisfied with me. We'll be on winter vacation from December 28th and perhaps I'll travel to visit our parents.

Do your best to send us a detailed letter by then. Here work is bubbling, and we're readying for the forthcoming elections.

There's nothing new with me. I've joined a very good family. The wife is a *balabusta*, a wonderful homemaker; she's also a teacher and I eat lunch there, so it worked out very well. I'm looking forward to a postcard from Tzeka** and I'll write to him too. Be well and write more frequently,

Yours,

Lena

Vilna

Diminutive for Yehezkel

Lena Klebanovila
Gedimino
RS

***

Vilnius, 1 December 1940

MY DEAR BROTHER,

I'd have written to you long ago but I kept waiting for a postcard from you. On 20 November I received a postcard from Luba saying that one was also sent to you on 8 November, in which he states that you'll also write to me, which is why I waited. He wrote saying that he also sent a postcard to our parents but they haven't received it yet.

Now that you're working at the factory I'm very happy. I thought you were with him, and wrote to our parents that I received a telegram response. I also advised them by postcard. You'd probably find it hard to understand their joy. Their response letter is here with me. What's going on with me you already know. I'm working at the government high school, teaching Lithuanian language to grades 5, 6 and 7. I'm earning well and pleased with the work. The school is also pleased with me.

I'm living with very intelligent people, and also eat there. All we're missing now is both of you. You can't imagine how worried our parents are about you, but otherwise they feel quite well. We still haven't begun the harsh winter. It's only started getting cold. On the 28th we went on winter vacation and it may be that I'll go home for a few days because I haven't seen our parents since the start of the school year.

How are things at your end? How are you managing with work? What answer did the Russian Consulate provide? Is there any hope that you'll be able to return? It's now our only dream and it looks like it's yours too and will come true.

As for our socialist homeland, a Jew no longer has to travel to find work in foreign countries because anyone who truly wants work can find it here.

I'm strongly requesting now that you answer my postcard and write to our parents too.

All the best,

Your sister,

Lena

Lena Klebanovite
Gedimino, Vilnius, Lithuania

Postcard shows the ancient city of Kaunus (Kovno), Soviet Republic of Lithuania:

Boats at sea. Vilnus St. Etienne
Vilna, 14 December 1940

MY DEAR LITTLE BROTHER,

I received a letter from home which also contained your postcard, and later received your other postcards. You can't even imagine how happy that makes me. Rubin came over and also told me he received a postcard from you.

After so many months of uncertainty!

It's such a great joy for all of us that I can't even describe it. Our parents also received a postcard from Luba. As you see all I need to do now is answer, which is exactly what I'm doing! Let us know how things are going with your papers.*

Rubin said that you've probably already read this, but we start winter break on 23 December so I'll be seeing our parents quite soon. Write to them more often because it's the only real joy they have, receiving letters from you both.

Nothing is new with me. I'm working and happy with my job. Stay well. Why didn't you send regards with Gershonov when you wrote to Rubin?

L. Klebanov
49/1 St. Etienne

* *Official government documents*

***

Till his dying day Abba kept his sister's letters. I still have some of the postcards; others I donated to Yad Vashem, the World Holocaust Center in Jerusalem. The letters I kept describe everyday life, which today is a precious asset linking the home in Vandžiogala with the utter eradication of the town's residents and all that it encompassed.

I'm proud of Abba for having lived a full life after the loss, for having established a family and earning a livelihood worthy of respect, and for finding time for photography. I learned from him that we should never stop trying, producing, and clowning around even if we're sad.

Thank you, Abba. My writing is a kind of 'Tikkun Olam,' a rectification to our world.

In memory of my Zeideh, my Bobbeh and my Aunt the lives and souls of Frieda, Haim and Lena Klebanov were snuffed out, but their immortal souls nonetheless live on in ours.

In memory of my father, Yehezkel: whose narrow shoulders found it hard to bear the suffering but who went smiling into that world where all is good, welcomed by his beloved brother, his sister Lena, his parents, a hundred or so neighbors from his hometown, a very tall turkey, and a goat with a golden bell. Doffing his rakishly and elegantly angled Borsellino, he waved goodbye and, finally, at last, ceased worrying.

In memory of my uncle, Leon: whose Hebrew name was Aryeh Nahum, the lion, the comfort. Uncle Leon passed away in Paris at a ripe old age. He carried on his narrow shoulders years of guilt for his family's suffering. He departed, smiling, moving in light dance-like steps into that world where all is good, and met his wife, her five-year-old son and mother who were murdered in France, and he met his brother and their family, and some hundred neighbors from his hometown, a turkey that ate from their table, and a white goat. He nodded in greeting to them all, and finally, at last, ceased worrying.

In memory of my brother, Avinoam Klebanov, who passed away at a very young age.

In memory of the Vandžiogala community, and the Jews of Lithuania.

EPILOGUE

As I approached the end of this writing expedition, I joined the 'Vilna Origins Organization' trip to Lithuania, traveling by plane, on foot and, in the bus, where we could all sigh deeply. The shock paralyzed us.

We stood in silence at Punar, listening to Mrs. Branchowski talk in Yiddish about joining the ghetto's underground, then the avenging partisans group in the Rudniki Forest under the command of Abba (Abel) Kovner. We listened to the commander of the underground, the now late Dr. Aharon Einat (Zelkin), describe their hideout. These warriors' dignity remained steadfast when faced with the misery meted out to the innocents who were never able to fight or hide. Some of us bowed our heads, others cried, some were silent, their silence deafening.

After that trip, my perspective altered. A gray cloud settled around me. Had I waited to begin writing until after this trip, I would have found it close to impossible to write this book, replete with innocence and color.

***

The war in Lithuania is known as a 'close contact war.' There were no crematoria. Instead, Jews were meticulously murdered, one by one. Here's how they did it: young girls were shot in the leg to make them limp all the way into the mass graves; Jews were slaughtered, mocked, burnt, massacred, beheaded, and buried alive.

My family's neighbors, fascists, were the ones who killed my family.

Rivers in Lithuania ran red.

***

I presumed that the Klebanovs lived not far from the synagogue. When we asked a local where the synagogue had stood, he glared at us with a razor-sharp stare, his pupils looked like a pair of guns. After making such a tremendous effort to find and reach Vandžiogala, I hadn't been prepared for that kind of reaction. I could barely breathe. I desperately needed oxygen. I asked Danny, our group guide, if we could leave the town.

Desecration is everywhere in the Jewish cemetery in Vandžiogala. We walk along a muddy path through bits of broken headstones, piles of cow manure and broken vodka bottles. The local Lithuanians wouldn't even let the long-since dead rest in peace.

I thought about fencing the cemetery. I was told there was no point. The fence would be broken, possibly even recycled for other uses.

This book is my fence, my testimony to the family that once filled a significant spot in Vandžiogala's community and in Lithuanian Jewry.

The Gray Cloud

If a turkey could talk
Perhaps it'd talk about my Zeideh, my Bobbeh, my aunt,
About Lithuanians who invaded my family's home,
About the neighbors who looted, robbed, murdered,
About Bobbeh Frieda who I never had and she never had me,
About conversations, get-togethers,
hugs that were never shared,
About the heart-rending absence, the painful nothingness,
The loss that catches like a vise, that punctures the routine,
That turns it into a grayish lace.

The turkey living in my Bobbeh's house bowed its head
at the horrors,
Unable to sound its gob-gob-gobble.

Through Yiddish, which I'm now learning,
I rediscover the lost melodies, the sharp humor.
Zeideh, Bobbeh and my aunt would likely have loved to chat
with me in Yiddish.
If we ever do meet again, even in some other universe,
We would probably prefer to sit close to each other, sip tea,
and be silent together.

This book is a tribute to my perished family.
To the white goat with its golden bell,
And to the turkey so tall it could eat from the table.

The memory has not disappeared.
It is alive and well.

THROUGH MY EYES

This book was born of longing.

A Yad Vashem 'testimonial page' is the only thing left of Frieda Klebanov. Bobbeh Frieda and her family, my family, perished seven years before I was born, wordlessly, without eulogy. Her death seeped into my veins.

Memory and imagination overcome the laws of logic.

Frieda and I meet via thought, art and this book.

The book does not follow a chronology of events. Who would even put their faith in such orderliness? The story follows the way I see things, including the invisible. It is a story made up of windows, slivers of memories, the little that Abba told me, and a great many more shards which I sensed he kept hidden or was unable to talk about. And so I set about embroidering them into a quilt, like the artist and art therapist that I am, using glue and collage.

My friends are accustomed to my manner of thought and speech.

"One second," I say, "let me open brackets."

"Will you remember to come back?"

"Yes."

As though participating in a mathematical equation, I've become used to opening small parentheses, larger brackets, always remembering to come back to where the detour began.

THINKING LIKE WINDOWS

Some of our generation suffers from attention deficit disorders, some of us think like Google, some like Windows, every other moment opening new brackets, checking data, opening smaller brackets, a window, a door, a slit, an aperture, and the main thing is not to forget to return to where we started. It's our zigzaggy way of thinking.

Frieda Klebanov (left) and her daughter Lena

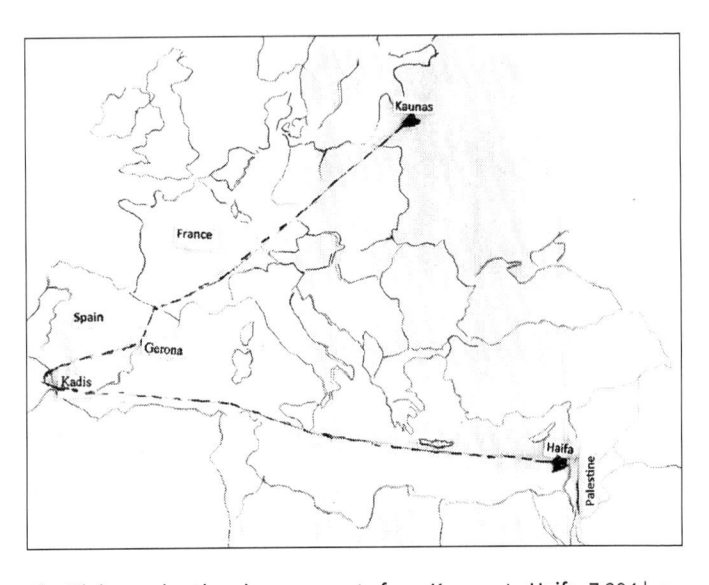

The Klebanov brothers' escape route from Kaunas to Haifa: 7,294 km

1927: The brothers leave home for studies in France

1941: Fleeing from France to Spain

1942: 9 months in Gerona Prison as POW

February 1944: Loaded with European refugees, "Niassa" sails to Haifa, Palestine

CHAGALL

The book links images and stories, connecting the fantastical figures hovering in the blue heaven in Chagall's paintings to the rusty food graters floating in the sky in Yosl Bergner's artwork.

This book is a tribute to my family members who are no more
But they did not live in vain.
Between the lines you and I infuse them with new life, and not just on the page.

I cannot patch up that which is torn or fill in gaps but, as the mother of five and grandmother of a baker's dozen, I hope to transmit to the next generation the beads of the chain. Let us remain attentive, let us know whence we came and where we are heading and, on the journey, let us not forget to dream, to write, to read, to create, to invent worlds.

Creative work need not take into consideration the rules of gravity and chronology, otherwise how can what truly happened on those murky days, which cracked us apart, ever be described if not in some fantastical manner?

CHAPTER TWO

As time passed and I myself became a grandmother, I wove a make-believe saga. In it, Frieda feels what may eventuate, encourages her family to leave the home and they as well as the goat fly on the turkey's back, saving them all, bringing them to the Land of Israel.

The fantasy and the dream add dimensions of expanded time to my reality.

A WONDROUS JOURNEY ON THE TURKEY'S BACK

When Frieda opened the door, she saw a very tall turkey.

A grand creature, it waddled over to the table and gobbled up a cube of sugar.

"Hey! Pardon me! Exactly what's going on here?" Frieda exclaimed, taken by surprise.

The turkey, hungry and exhausted, looked at her with a sorrowful gaze.

Frieda cleared a corner in the room. The turkey clucked in gratitude, crumpled with a heavy thud, and instantly fell asleep.

Lena returned from school.

"Mama," she asked, "what is that strange sound? Gob-gob-gobble?"

Frieda hesitated, choosing her words. "It's a wonderful turkey. He'll rest here, for now."

Two days passed. Frieda opened the door and saw, standing there, a gaunt goat. She tied a golden bell around its neck and led it to the yard. The goat grinned.

"Theh-eh-eh-eh-ehnk you," it said, then lowered its head to graze on the grass.

Lena returned from school.

"Mama," she asked, "what's that strange sound? Ding-dong, meh-meh?"

Frieda hesitated, choosing her words. "It's a cute, hungry goat. She'll rest here, for now."

The hours passed. Frieda's heart felt premonitions of evil.

"Tomorrow, Lena, you won't go to school. And you, Haim, won't go to work. This very night we must flee. A terrible, furious storm is about to break out!"

"Mama, what could possibly happen? And what about the animals?"

"Lena, my sweetie, don't worry, we'll find a solution," her mother reassured.

Deep in the night, they shut the door, opened the gate, set out single file, walking incredibly quickly: Haim, Frieda, Lena, the white goat, and the tall turkey, a pack of food tied to his back.

Winds blew fiercely, thunder growled loudly, lightning flashed boldly. They huddled together, trembling.

"Don't worry," Frieda said, "this very night we'll cross the border."

The next day they were very hungry. They each ate a handful of lentils. And so they slowly walked, single file: Haim, Frieda, Lena, the tall turkey, and the white goat, a pack of food tied to her back.

Suddenly a strange gobbling sound was heard. "Friends, it is almost midnight and we must cross several borders. Climb onto my back now, and we will rise up and fly," said the turkey.

"That's an impossible task," the father worried. "We'll be too heavy."

But Frieda whispered. "The turkey's right. We need to be daring!"

And so, they climbed on: Haim, then Frieda, but Lena wondered, "What about the goat?"

"White goat, don't be scared. Quickly, climb onto my back," encouraged the turkey.

Lena and the goat clambered on, took their seats, and the turkey clucked, spread its wings, and slowly, slowly rose into the sky.

"Mama! Mama!" Lena called. "It's unbelievable! We're soaring! In a moment we'll be in the clouds."

"Lena, my sweet girl, it's best to be quiet because things still aren't safe.

"Hold on tight!" the turkey cried out, "and hold onto each other, we're going further up now!"

The earth shook, rogue waves leapt higher, flares singed the treetops, thick slate-gray smoke pillared upwards from chimney stacks, lightning, thunder, terrible jolts, chaos, the most frightening scene ever.

"I knew it," Frieda whispered. "Indeed, a mighty, terrible storm has broken out." Meanwhile, the storm destroys forests, people, animals, and homes in its wake.

High in the sky a golden moon watched the first star begin to sparkle. Lena did not fall asleep. Frieda worried.

"Hold on, hold on!" the turkey called out again. "We're about to cross the borders. Don't worry, I know some secret paths. Trust me, my friends. I see far into the distance; very, very far."

Between the clouds this wondrous group flew on the

back of the robust turkey: Haim, Frieda, Lena, the white goat, with a pack of food tied to her back.

They passed over countries and lakes, their journey taking many days. The goat suddenly opened her eyes and bleated.

"Hey! Look, we've crossed the border!"

Haim was the first to react. "What a relief to have the flood and fury behind us."

"Mama, Tateh, look!" Lena was excited. "There, in the heart of the sea. A boat!"

"Hold on tight, friends. We're diving down!" the turkey laughed in a loud, rolling cackle.

Surprised and confused, they landed on the deck. Luckily for them the captain greeted them warmly.

"Wonderful people, what happened? You look awful! But thank God, we're sailing to the Land of Israel."

And so they arrived, safe and sound, on the shores of Tel Aviv: Haim, with Lena on his shoulders; Frieda, Haim's arm holding her firmly; the goat's hair turned gray, and the turkey was exhausted to the roots of his quills. Under the sun's warm rays the little convoy strode, tired but thrilled.

"I'll let you in on a secret. In a moment we'll see Uncle Nimrod," Frieda announced.

When Nimrod opened the door, he noticed the wonderful procession.

"How incredible!" he said. "Come in. Come on in. A miracle from heaven. I heard terrible rumors: that entire communities had disappeared, but what luck that Frieda's so smart. You've fled right on time. What an inspiring little group."

"Thank you, Nimrod, for your hospitality," Haim said.

After a much-need rest, they ate and spent hours telling of their wondrous journey among the clouds, way above the cresting waves, how they fled the Divine's storm, about the dangers and challenges. Even before they finished telling the tale, they all fell fast asleep: Haim, Frieda, Lena, the white goat, and the extremely tired turkey.

At midnight Frieda startled awake.

"Was I just dreaming, or were we really saved by a wonder-filled journey?"

IN THEIR MEMORY

My grandfather, the leader of his community, went to his death.

Although his wife and daughter knew their end was near, Zeideh felt he was responsible for the community and refused to flee.

My Zeideh's family and their neighbors stepped in silence to the valley of killing.

If only the turkey could talk…

Maybe, just maybe, they could have had a different ending.

Printed by Amazon Italia Logistica S.r.l.
Torrazza Piemonte (TO), Italy